AMELIA FANG
and the
UNICORN LORDS

LAURA ELLEN ANDERSON

EGMONT

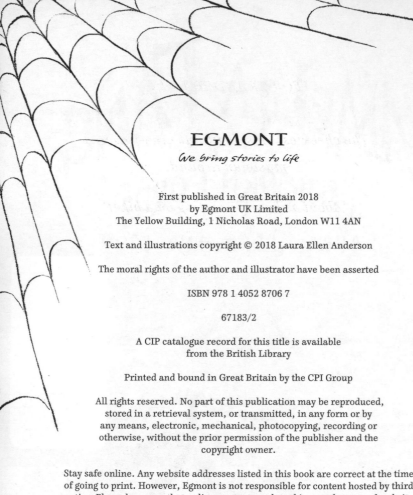

EGMONT

We bring stories to life

First published in Great Britain 2018
by Egmont UK Limited
The Yellow Building, 1 Nicholas Road, London W11 4AN

Text and illustrations copyright © 2018 Laura Ellen Anderson

The moral rights of the author and illustrator have been asserted

ISBN 978 1 4052 8706 7

67183/2

A CIP catalogue record for this title is available
from the British Library

Printed and bound in Great Britain by the CPI Group

Stay safe online. Any website addresses listed in this book are correct at the time
of going to print. However, Egmont is not responsible for content hosted by third
parties. Please be aware that online content can be subject to change and websites
can contain content that is unsuitable for children. We advise that all children
are supervised when using the internet.

MIX
Paper from
responsible sources
FSC® C020471

FOR GRANDAD JOHN

The cheekiest most brilliant nine-fingered

musician around.

'About as handy as a frog on a bike!'

Love you always.

Twiglett xxx

CONTENTS

MAP OF NOCTURNIA viii

MEET THE NOCTURNIANS AND

GLITTEROPOLANS x

1. WHY DO I 'AVE TO BE THE UNICORN? . . 1

2. THE WISHING WELL OF WELL

   WISHES 17

3. PUMPKIN POO 29

4. McSPARKLE 41

5. THE ETERNAL HUG 51

6. RAINBOOOOW! 63

7. FABIO 75

8. GLITTEROPOLIS 87

9. COLLAR DUSTER 101

10. THE HAUNTED HOUSE RIDE 115

11. STRONG INDEPENDENT UNICORN . . . 129

12. THE UNICORN BANQUET 139

13. FLORENCE'S UNIQUE TALENT 151

14. THE CANDY CHAMBERS 161

15. FLORENCE IS NOT A BEAST 177

16. A TICKLE BEHIND THE EAR 185

17. LEPRECHAUNS ASSEMBLE 201

18. LIGHT AND DARK 211

Ghoulish Greetings from . . .

AMELIA AND SQUASHY

LIKES:
Hugs and Tongue
Twister sandwiches

DISLIKES:
Going to bed early

TANGINE

LIKES:
His new friends,
Amelia, Florence
and Grimaldi

DISLIKES:
An empty stomach

FLORENCE AND GRIMALDI

LIKES:
Adventures with Amelia

DISLIKES:
Rude wishing wells

KING VLADIMIR

LIKES:
Dungeons and Daymares game

DISLIKES:
Slimescale in the kettle

FAIRYWEATHER

LIKES:
Glitter and family

DISLIKES:
Runaway Mushrooms

McSPARKLE

LIKES:
Jigging and
rainbows

DISLIKES:
Fuzzmites

FABIO

LIKES:
Strong Independent Unicorns

DISLIKES:
Creatures of the Dark

CHAPTER 1

WHY DO I 'AVE TO BE THE UNICORN?

SQUEEEEEEEEEEEEEEEEEEEEEEEEE! squeeed the pumpkin alarm clock at first light.

Amelia Fang stretched and scrambled out of her coffin. Her pet pumpkin Squashy was bouncing around licking everyone excitedly.

'Oh, Squashy,' Amelia said through a yawn, 'how are you so wide awake?'

'SQUISH EVERYTHING!' moaned Florence Spudwick, rolling over. Florence was a huge, rare breed of yeti, *not* to be confused with a beast. She was also one of Amelia's best friends.

'It can't be time already?' Grimaldi groaned, pulling his hood over his face. Grimaldi Reaperton was Death himself. But until he was older, he only dealt with the deaths of small creatures in Nocturnia, leaving the bigger creatures to his grimpapa.

It was the Halloween holidays and the sun had risen in the Kingdom of the Dark, which meant that every creature in Nocturnia and the scary suburbs would be going to bed – apart from Amelia Fang and her friends. They were about to embark on a very big quest to the Kingdom of the Light.

'FLORENCE!' said Prince Tangine La Floofle the First, clapping his hands twice. 'I demand breakfast!'

'DON'T *CLAP* ME!' said Florence, clenching her big hairy fists.

'Tangine,' Amelia said with a sigh, 'remember what we discussed. *Try* not to be so bossy.'

'I keep forgetting,' said Tangine sheepishly. 'Can't I be a *leeeettle* bit bossy?'

'No!' Amelia laughed. 'We're your *friends*.'

'Maids.' Tangine smiled.

'*Fur-riends*,' said Amelia.

Tangine took a deep breath. 'Fuuur . . .' He wiped his forehead. 'Fuuur . . .' he tried again. '*Fuuurmaids?*' He looked proud of himself.

'That's . . . progress,' Amelia said.

When Amelia had first met Tangine, he had been quite mean to her and had stolen her pet pumpkin, Squashy. But it had turned out that Prince Tangine had been lonely and just wanted a friend. Tangine had grown up all alone in the palace with only Mummy Maids for company. He did have a mother – she was a fairy named Fairyweather. Tragically, Fairyweather had mysteriously disappeared when Tangine was just a baby. Prince

Tangine's father, King Vladimir, had been so sad about his wife's disappearance that he had neglected his kingdom and Tangine, spending years searching in vain for her. This meant that not only had Tangine grown into rather a spoilt sprout (which was why he thought that it was perfectly OK to steal poor Squashy) but also that he was half-vampire, half-fairy. This big secret of Tangine's was something that would have terrified most Creatures of the Dark. But Amelia had discovered that Creatures of the Light weren't as scary as they had all been told. It turns out that fairies did *not* steal your fangs and unicorns did *not* shoot killer rainbows from their bottoms.

'I'm so tired, I'm not sure I can cope with being awake during the day,' said Grimaldi.

'We'll get used to it,' Amelia reassured him.

As Amelia and her friends made their way

along the corridor of the Fang Mansion, an eruption of laughter came from below, followed by a large belch. Amelia's dad, Count Drake the Third, slowly floated bottom-first out of the dining room and up towards the ceiling.

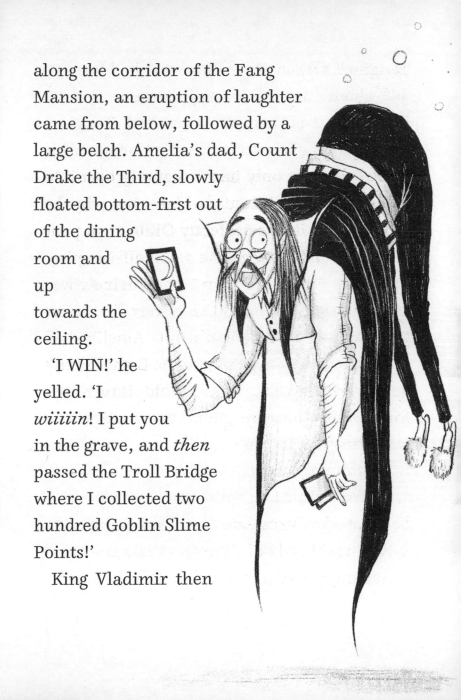

'I WIN!' he yelled. 'I *wiiiiin*! I put you in the grave, and *then* passed the Troll Bridge where I collected two hundred Goblin Slime Points!'

King Vladimir then

swayed into view with a hiccup. He also began to float up towards the ceiling. 'INCORRECT, Drake, me ol' knee-flapper!' *BELCH*. 'I was ON the Troll Bridge *way* before you got there because I used my Wolf Howl card combined with the Lightning Bolt bonus point I'd saved up . . .'

'You both lose,' called Amelia's mum, Countess Frivoleeta. 'I got the Total Eclipse card. *LOOK!*' She waved an elaborate-looking card in front of their faces.

'Bother!' said the count and King Vladimir together. They hugged each other and slowly rotated 360 degrees, before floating back down to ground level.

'*Muuuum!*' called Amelia from upstairs. 'It's first light. Didn't you realise?'

'*Creeping crevices*, you're right!' the countess shrieked. 'We got carried away playing Dungeons and Daymares! I can't believe it's that time already!' The adults clambered up the stairs.

King Vladimir had cheered up a lot since Amelia and her friends offered to help search for Fairyweather. He'd been searching alone for so long. Now he had help, and more importantly, *hope*.

In preparation for their risky quest to the Kingdom of the Light, the countess had made Amelia, Florence, Grimaldi and the king clever disguises to wear on their travels. As far as the Creatures of the Light were still concerned, vampires sucked their blood and yetis crushed their bones.

Squashy, disguised as a big daisy, pa-doinged

in excitement while Amelia gave a little twirl in her fairy costume.

'It's not bad . . .' she said, admiring her glittery wings. 'But aren't I a bit big to be a fairy?'

'Nonsense!' said the king. 'Fairies come in all shapes and sizes. Some rather large, and some teeny-weeny. My Fairyweather was about the length of my arm. A great size for hugging,' he said with a smile.

'WHY DO I 'AVE TO BE THE UNICORN?'

said Florence, straightening her horn as Grimaldi studied his angel-kitten tail nervously.

Tangine admired his (real) fairy wings in one of the countess's many mirrors. 'I think I look AMAZING!' he exclaimed. 'Dad, did you ever dress in disguise when you used to travel to the Kingdom of the Light on your own?'

'I tried,' said the king. 'But I had nobody to help me and I'm *terrible* at sewing. I *tried* to make a unicorn costume myself, but it fell apart en route to the Fairy Forest and I was left

stranded . . . how do I put this?' The king paused. 'Completely nude.'

Everybody erupted with laughter. 'KING IN THE NUD!' Florence bellowed. Then she punched the wall and dented it.

'Yes, yes, calm down,' said the king, his normally pale cheeks flushed.

'But . . . couldn't the Mummy Maids have helped make you a disguise?' said Amelia through snorts of laughter.

'PAH!' It was the king's turn to chortle. 'Have you ever seen a Mummy Maid try to use

a sewing machine? They'd sew their heads together!'

'Don't fear, your highness, this time I've made you the perfect disguise, and I promise it won't fall apart.' The countess beamed. She handed the king a pair of spotty wings.

'Um . . .' The king looked awkwardly at the disguise. 'Is that a ladybird costume?'

'Correct!' Countess Frivoleeta smiled and curtseyed. 'A terrifying ladybird costume!'

She looked very proud of herself.

'I may be a *tad* large to pass as a ladybird,' murmured the king, pulling his costume on.

Youuuu aaaare dead, you are dead! Grimaldi's diePhone rang out from his pocket, letting him know some poor creature needed his services.

'I'm not sure you'll get a signal while we're in the Kingdom of the Light,' said the king. 'Your grimpapa says he'll make sure any squished toads are taken care of while you're away.'

'Thank you, your majesty,' said Grimaldi, handing the diePhone to Countess Frivoleeta for safe keeping.

The countess put it in her pocket, then wrapped Amelia in her arms. The scent of her

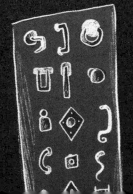

mother's new Slug Slime-Trail perfume was overpowering. 'Oh, Amelia. Be safe out there, won't you?'

'I will, Mum, don't worry.' Amelia smiled.

'YEH, WE GOT A MASSIVE LADYBIRD TO KEEP US SAFE!' Florence chuckled.

'And if you see *any* crossword puzzles in the Kingdom of the Light, do bring some back. I love a new challenge!' said the count.

'Now, Tangine, do you have the map of the Kingdom of the Light?' said the king.

'I gave it to Florence because she likes maps.' Tangine blushed.

'DON'T WORRY, I'M KEEPIN' IT SAFE,' replied Florence. 'ROLLED IT UP ALL NICE INSIDE MY UNICORN 'ORN.'

'Excellent!' said the king. Then, from inside

his ladybird wing, he pulled out a scrap of glittery parchment: the clue he had found in the Petrified Forest the night Queen Fairyweather had gone missing.

It read:

'**GLITTEROPOLIS, the city where the sun never goes down, and your dreams always come true . . .**'

'Let's go and find Glitteropolis!' said the king.

'Now, where's the right door?' asked the countess.

The doors in the Fang Mansion tended to move around a lot. It was a matter of skill – and a dollop of good luck – to know which door led where.

'Here it is,' she announced, gesturing to a wooden door covered with vines. 'If I remember correctly, this should lead you to the edge of

the Petrified Forest, and according to the king's map—'

'THE KINGDOM OF LIGHT BORDERS THE FOREST,' Florence finished proudly.

'Well, here goes,' said Amelia, opening the door. She reached up to her head and gave Squashy a reassuring pat.

King Vladimir ruffled Tangine's hair. 'Come on, son, let's go and find Mum!'

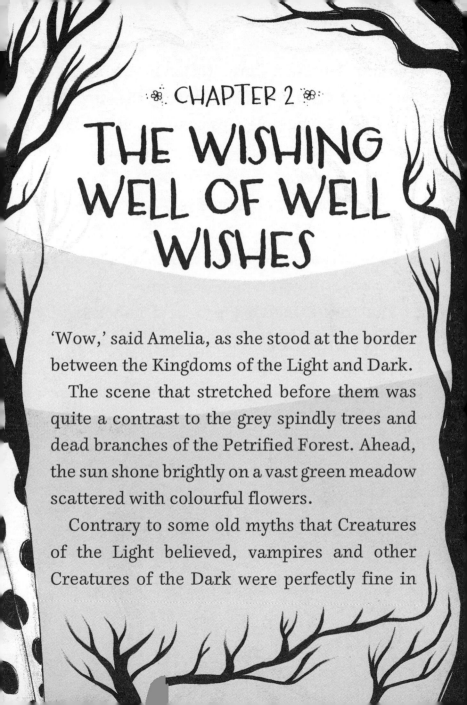

CHAPTER 2

THE WISHING WELL OF WELL WISHES

'Wow,' said Amelia, as she stood at the border between the Kingdoms of the Light and Dark.

The scene that stretched before them was quite a contrast to the grey spindly trees and dead branches of the Petrified Forest. Ahead, the sun shone brightly on a vast green meadow scattered with colourful flowers.

Contrary to some old myths that Creatures of the Light believed, vampires and other Creatures of the Dark were perfectly fine in the sun. They just weren't used to it, since they were usually fast asleep during the day. The soft hum of bumblebees made Amelia feel a little uneasy. Grimaldi yelped as a bunny rabbit hopped into view.

'The Meadow of Loveliness . . .' said King Vladimir.

Amelia took a deep breath. 'Are we all ready?' she said, straightening herself up.

The friends nodded and held hands tightly before stepping for the first time into the Kingdom of the Light.

Amelia gasped as her foot sank into the soft ground. It felt strange and spongy. The long grass was shimmering and even the air seemed to be sparkling. But it wasn't as awful as she might have expected – just *very* different.

'*Flaaarg!*' Grimaldi shrieked as a butterfly tried to land on his head. 'It's going to eat me!'

'*Grimaldi!*' hissed Amelia. 'You'll draw

attention to us!'

'YEH. YOU NEED TO BE MORE CREATUREY OF THE LIGHTY,' said Florence. 'MAYBE WE SHOULD PRANCE,' she continued. 'THEY LIKE TO PRANCE, RIGHT?'

Without waiting for a reply, Florence pirouetted across the flowerbeds as if she were as light as a feather.

Amelia noticed Tangine's mouth drop open as he watched Florence dance among the flowers. She was quite surprised herself.

'She's quite the prancer!' said the king with a laugh, before attempting a skip, hop and jump. He stopped when he pulled a muscle in his back.

'Not as nimble as I used to be . . .' he said, wincing.

Amelia felt a little nervous, but then she began shuffling her feet. And, before she knew it, she found herself skipping through the long grass. 'Come on, Grimaldi! It's fun!' she called.

Grimaldi stood frozen to the spot. Amelia ran over and grabbed both his hands, pulling him into the meadow.

'*Eeeeeeeeeek!*' Grimaldi squealed. 'I think something flew into my mouth!'

'There's nothing to fear, Grimaldi!' the king reassured him. '*Look*, the Creatures of the Light are just getting on with their lives.' He pointed at a small bunny rabbit nibbling on some grass.

'I dunno,' Grimaldi mumbled, 'maybe it's plotting something terrible as we speak . . .'

'Oh, you are silly!' Amelia giggled.

'Look, Dad!' Tangine yelled. 'I'm flying!' Tangine was hovering a few feet above the grass, his sparkly fairy wings flapping fiercely.

'You look just like your mother!' King

Vladimir said, smiling.

'THIS PLACE ISN'T SO BAD,' said Florence, performing one last pirouette.

'Right,' said the king, 'let's check the map and work out our best route.'

Florence took the unicorn horn off her head and removed the map, which was neatly rolled into a cone.

'Where do we start?' said Grimaldi as Florence straightened the map out. 'We have no idea where Glitteropolis city is – it's not on the map.'

'Hey look, there's the Wishing Well of Well Wishes,' said Amelia, reading the map. 'Maybe we could make a wish to find out where Glitteropolis is?'

'Amelia, that is

a great idea. I'd never thought of that before!'
The king beamed. Then he looked at Tangine
fondly. 'The Wishing Well of Well Wishes is
where your mum and I got married.'

The friends waded through the Meadow of
Loveliness, stopping every so often for King
Vladimir to catch his breath.

'At least I'll be fitter by the time we find
Fairyweather,' he puffed.

'That must be the Wishing Well of Well
Wishes!' said Grimaldi, pointing ahead at a
stone well. It appeared to be glowing, and
sparkly flecks of light danced around its rim.

Florence peered into the well and shouted,
''OW DO YOU MAKE A WISH THEN?'

THEN. . .

THEN. . .

THEN. . .

Her voice echoed.

'NO NEED TO SHOUT!' a voice boomed up from within the well.

SPLOSH!

A huge jet of water followed, drenching Florence from head to toe.

'IT SPLOSHED ME!' said Florence in shock. 'AND IT SPOKE.'

'I'll do it again if you don't stop referring to me as *IT*, you big oaf,' said the voice from the well.

There was no doubt about it: the Wishing Well of Well Wishes could talk. And it was really rather rude.

'So, what brings you Creatures of the Dark to the Kingdom of the Light?' asked the well.

Everyone looked at each other in surprise. How could it have seen through their disguises?

'W-w-we're not Creatures of the Dark!' said Grimaldi quickly. 'Look! *Meeeow!*' And he swung his angel-kitten tail around.

'Do you think I'm completely blind, little grim reaper?' said the well.

'COURSE YOU ARE,' Florence cut in, ''CAUSE YOU 'AVE NO EYES.'

SPLOSH!

Tangine stifled a giggle as Florence received another face full of water.

'All right, Vlad?' said the well. 'Or should I say, Sir Ladybird?'

'I see you haven't changed,' said the king

raising an eyebrow.

'And I see your son is growing up to look just like his mother,' said the well. 'Got your nose, though . . . Shame.'

'How do you know so much about us?' asked Tangine. 'You're just a wishing well.'

'I am *the* Wishing Well of Well Wishes! I know everything there is to know and everything that will be known.'

'I KNOW YOU'RE PRETTY RUDE,' said Florence.

'Don't take it personally,' whispered the king. 'Wells are notorious for being a little *uncouth* at times.'

'If you know everything, then can you tell us where Glitteropolis is?' said Amelia.

'Maybe,' said the well.

'You just told us you *know everything*,' said Amelia.

'I do,' said the well.

'Then surely you know where the city of Glitteropolis is?' said Amelia, becoming impatient.

'Yes,' said the well.

'Then *can't you tell us*?'

'I can't,' said the well.

'Why not?' Grimaldi cried.

'I don't just *give out* information. I'm not allowed to. So, the secret of who you are is safe with me. Unless someone *wishes* to know your secret, that is . . .' The well coughed. 'But anyway, if you want information, you must *wish* for it,' said the well.

'I *WISH* YOU'D JUST STOP TALKING!' Florence blurted out, clenching her fists.

'No, Flo—' the king began.

But the well bubbled and a small envelope

came hurtling through the air landing at Florence's feet. She picked up the envelope and opened it.

PFFFFFFFFFFFFTTT!

'AAAARGH!' Florence bellowed as the envelope exploded into a cloud of glitter. The glitter-cloud then rearranged itself to spell out:

THANK YOU FOR YOUR FIRST WISH.
WE HOPE IT WAS FULFILLED TO YOUR
EXPECTATIONS.

Then the glitter words disappeared.

'WHAT? I DIDN'T MAKE A WISH!' yelled Florence.

But the well was silent. It made no sound, not even a bubble.

CHAPTER 3

PUMPKIN POO

Amelia put her head in her hands. 'I think you did make a wish, Florence. You wished the well would *stop talking*.'

'THAT WASN'T A PROPER WISH!' said Florence.

'You have to be extra careful with what you say,' explained the king.

The well was still silent.

'I guess we need to wish for the well to speak again?' said Tangine looking to his dad.

'Hmmm, it does seem like the only way,' the king said.

'ALL RIGHT. FINE,' said Florence. 'I WISH THE WELL WOULD SPEAK AGAIN . . .'

Another small envelope came hurtling from inside the well, landing at Florence's feet, and then exploding into a cloud of glitter spelling out the words:

THANK YOU FOR YOUR SECOND WISH.
WE HOPE IT WAS FULFILLED TO YOUR
EXPECTATIONS.

'Well done,' said the well. 'You just wasted two of your three wishes. It's the standard three wish rule and you speak for everyone here, yeti.'

'I AM NOT—' Florence began. 'OH, WAIT. I AM A YETI.' She trailed off.

'*Guuuys*, we only have *one* wish left!' said Grimaldi, twizzling his angel-kitten tail nervously. 'We should ask about Glitteropolis!'

'WELL, 'IS MAJESTY NEEDS TO FIND 'IS WIFE, RIGHT?' said Florence. 'SO . . .'

'Perhaps *someone else* should make this wish, Florence,' said Amelia warily.

'I agree, I can make this w—' the king began.

'I GOT THIS,' Florence interrupted and stomped up to the edge of the well. 'I WISH KING VLADIMIR WOULD—' Suddenly Florence began coughing and spluttering. '*BEEEE! A BEE!*' she choked. 'AAARGH! IT FLEW INTO ME MOUF!'

'Oh no, *Florence*,' stammered the king. 'What have you done?'

Florence spat and coughed. 'SORRY 'BOUT THAT. LEMME START AGAIN.'

But before Florence could carry on, an envelope came flying out of the well, landing at her feet with the usual glitter explosion.

THANK YOU FOR YOUR THIRD WISH.
WE HOPE IT WAS FULFILLED TO YOUR
EXPECTATIONS.

Then . . .

POOF!

The king disappeared into a puff of glittery smoke.

'*Pottering pumpkins!*' cried Amelia.

'WHERE'D THE KING GO?' said Florence.

'What did you do with my dad?' Tangine yelled into the well.

'We've wasted all the wishes!' Grimaldi had entered full-blown panic mode.

Where the king had been, a small bumble-bee perched on a flower.

'Florence! You turned the king into a BEE!' cried Amelia.

'BUT I DIDN'T! IT WAS THE WELL WHAT DID IT! I 'AD A BEE IN MY MOUF! MY WISH

GOT INTERRUPTED SO IT SHOUDN'T 'AVE BEEN GRANTED!' said Florence.

Tangine ran over to the bee. 'Dad?' he cried.

Buzzzzzzzzzzzzzz buzz buzzzzzz, buzzed the bee.

'*Daaaaaad!*' said Tangine. He tried to pick his dad up.

Buzzzzzzzzzzzzzz!

'Oh, Dad,' said Tangine. 'What do we do?'

The bee buzzed and then his little wings began vibrating and he flew away.

''E BUZZED OFF!' said Florence.

'Oh no! We're going to lose him!' said Amelia.

'What if he gets eaten or trampled on?' squealed Grimaldi, his eyes wide with panic.

Tangine started twiddling his thumbs. 'I've lost my mum *and* my dad now!' Then he stamped his foot angrily, creating a puff of glitter. 'How has this HAPPENED?'

'Please leave,' said the well calmly. 'Your wishes are complete. You must wait for one year before you can make another three wishes.'

'A YEAR?' said the friends in unison.

'That's the rule,' said the well.

'My dad can't be a bumblebee for *that* long!' whined Tangine, slumping down on to the grass.

Amelia sat down next to Tangine and put an arm around his shoulder. 'We'll work this out, I promise.'

'But *how*?' said Tangine sadly.

Amongst the long grass, Amelia caught sight of the piece of glittery parchment the king had kept hold of since Fairyweather's disappearance. She picked it up and tucked it safely behind one of her wings.

'I don't know right now, but *when* we find your mum, I'm sure she'll know what to do.' Amelia smiled.

Tangine nodded and took a deep breath.

'We can't carry on with this quest without the king!' said Grimaldi.

'We can, and we will,' said Amelia. 'We have each other and we have to work *together*.'

'NO FANKS TO THIS BIG PILE OF STONES.' Florence kicked at the side of the well.

Suddenly a huge SPLOSH of water

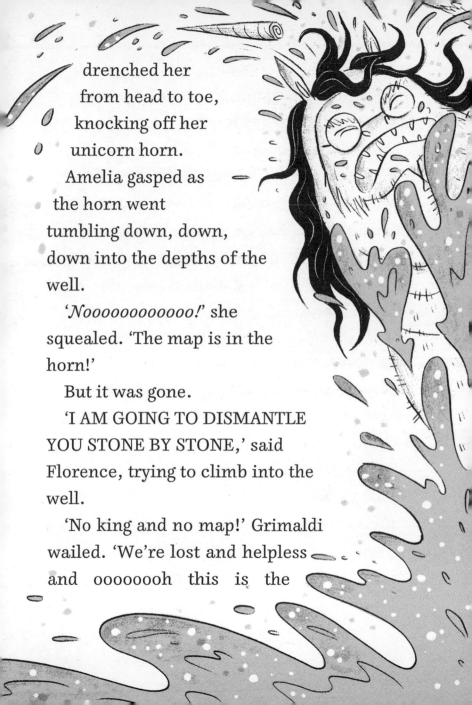

drenched her from head to toe, knocking off her unicorn horn.

Amelia gasped as the horn went tumbling down, down, down into the depths of the well.

'*Noooooooooooo!*' she squealed. 'The map is in the horn!'

But it was gone.

'I AM GOING TO DISMANTLE YOU STONE BY STONE,' said Florence, trying to climb into the well.

'No king and no map!' Grimaldi wailed. 'We're lost and helpless and oooooooh this is the ennnnnnd—'

Suddenly a spurt of water came flying out of the well, followed by Florence's unicorn horn.

'I am not a rubbish bin,' said the well. And then it sprinkled Grimaldi with water. 'And *you* are way too dramatic.'

'THE MAP!' Florence and Amelia cried. Amelia scooped up the dripping wet horn and pulled out the soaking map. It was now a big smudged mess.

'OH DEAR . . .' said Florence taking the map from Amelia. 'I'M SURE WE CAN FIX IT.' She wiped her paw across the sheet of parchment, making the smudge worse. It was no good. The map was ruined.

Grimaldi was breathing fast. 'We really should go back . . .'

Amelia stared at the ruined map, then screwed up her face. 'No!' she said firmly. 'We got this far. And we're here to find

Tangine's mum. And work out how to turn his dad back into a vampire. We must keep going, map or no map!'

'Please . . . leave . . .' said the well.

'BEFORE WE GO, I JUST NEED TO DO ONE THING,' said Florence.

The friends watched as Florence picked up Squashy and held him above the opening of the well. Amelia's heart leapt.

'Florence, *what are you—*'

Florence tickled Squashy's tummy and then – PARP.

He released a smelly little pumpkin poo, which fell into the depths of the well like a murky snowflake.

'MY WORK 'ERE IS DONE.' Florence grinned.

CHAPTER 4
McSPARKLE

Amelia and her friends carried on walking until they approached a forest. Squashy had got tired and **pa-doinged** up on top of Amelia's head. It was very different from the Petrified Forest back in Nocturnia, filled with a shimmering mist and beams of extra-bright sunlight. It took Amelia's vampire eyes a little while to adjust.

'I remember my dad saying something about a Fairy Forest,' said Tangine, studying his surroundings. 'This must be it.'

'Which way do we go from here?' said Grimaldi.

'I . . .' Amelia paused. 'I don't know.

Florence, what do you think?' she asked.

'WAIT A MINUTE. LET ME EYES ADJUST AND I'LL 'AV A FINK.' Florence said, rubbing her eyes, peering round a tree down another possible path. 'AAAARRRGH!' she cried suddenly. 'TANGINE, YOUR FACE! WHAT THE CABBAGE IS WRONG WIV YOUR FACE?'

But it wasn't Tangine that Florence had seen. Instead, a rosy-cheeked leprechaun wearing a bright-green hat walked past her and into the group.

'What *is* wrong with me face?' he said, looking offended.

Florence reached out to swat the leprechaun with her paw.

'STOP!' Amelia yelled. 'Florence . . . let's be *nice* to this kind *fellow Creature of the Light*!' she said through gritted teeth.

'Hello there!' said the leprechaun, skipping over to Amelia.

'Oh, hello!' She smiled. 'My friends and I are, err, on holiday here! I'm Amelia, by the way.'

'Well, isn't that grand?' said the leprechaun, tipping his hat. 'My name's McDonald Moonshine Misty Mountain Dew on a Summer's Morning Sparkle. But you can call me McSparkle.'

'Florence,' said a muffled voice.

'THAT'S AMAZING,' said Florence. 'MCSPARKLE JUST SPOKE WIVOUT MOVING 'IS MOUF! ARE YOU MAGIC?'

'No, Florence. That voice came from . . . *underneath* you,' said Amelia.

'*Florence!*' said the strained voice again.

'HOW AM I DOING THAT?' said Florence

peering downwards.

'Florence, you're *sitting* on Tangine!' said Grimaldi.

Florence lifted a bum cheek. 'OH, THERE YOU ARE.'

Tangine gasped for air.

McSparkle skipped over to Tangine and tipped his hat. 'So, what's your name, lad?'

While McSparkle and Tangine introduced themselves, Amelia whispered to

Florence and Grimaldi. 'Guys! McSparkle could be our answer to getting to Glitteropolis!'

'Did I hear the word *Glitteropolis*?' said McSparkle, popping up between Amelia and Florence.

'Do you know it? Our map is ruined, and we don't know how to get there,' said Amelia hopefully.

'I was just on me way to Glitteropolis!' said McSparkle.

'*REALLY*?' said Amelia, Florence, Grimaldi and Tangine together. Squashy squeaked in excitement. McSparkle looked at the top of Amelia's head in confusion.

'Could we come with you?' said Amelia, diverting his attention.

'Of course! It'll be nice to have some company!' McSparkle trilled. 'Been a tough few years, y'see. Me brother McShine went to the Delightful Docks to buy a new lute three summers ago and never returned.'

'That's awful,' said Amelia.

'Those *evil* Creatures of the Dark kidnapped him.' He frowned.

Florence grumbled. Grimaldi twirled his tail nervously.

'He's not the first Creature of the Light to go missing either,' said McSparkle, shaking his head.

'Fairyweather . . .' said Amelia without thinking.

'You knew her?' asked McSparkle.

'Quite well,' said Tangine, looking sad.

McSparkle looked around cautiously and then lowered his voice. 'We're not safe here any more,' he said. 'It's no wonder everyone's moving to Glitteropolis!'

Amelia nodded, pretending to agree.

'The Rainbow Rail is the best thing that's ever happened to this kingdom,' McSparkle continued, nodding wisely.

'Oh yes, I love the Rainbow Rail,' said Amelia. She had NO idea what the Rainbow Rail was. She'd never even seen a rainbow before – though she had read in a book about how they could blind you with their colours. 'It's so . . . rainbow-y.' She smiled nervously.

'There's no way Creatures of the Dark would ever guess the way into Glitteropolis is via a *rainbow*, eh?' McSparkle nudged Amelia's arm and chuckled.

That must be why King Vladimir could never find the city! thought Amelia.

'Right, folks,' McSparkle did a little heel click. 'We can catch the Rainbow Rail to Glitteropolis first thing tomorrow. It's a bit of a trek to the nearest rainbow stop from here, so we'll walk as far as we can before the sun sets, then make camp for the night. Let's go!'

When McSparkle was out of earshot, Amelia

threw her arms around Tangine. 'We did it!' she whispered happily. 'We're going to Glitteropolis! We're going to find your mum!' Then she paused. 'AND your dad . . .'

Tangine looked hesitant then smiled. 'You promise?' he whispered.

'I promise,' said Amelia. 'And friends don't break promises.'

CHAPTER 5
THE ETERNAL HUG

The beams of sunlight began to fade as evening approached in the Kingdom of the Light.

'Let's stop here for the night,' said McSparkle. 'We should collect some wood to make a fire before the light disappears.'

'Aww, look at the ickle fluffy mushroom,' Tangine cooed. He bent down to stroke what looked like a fluffy pink ball on the forest floor.

'*Don't touch that!*' shouted McSparkle. 'Didn't your mother ever tell you not to touch a fuzzmite?'

'She . . .' Tangine faltered. 'No. No she

didn't,' he said sadly.

'Well, don't touch 'em!' McSparkle frowned. 'Unless you want an eternal hug.'

'YEESH,' said Florence, surprised that a Creature of the Light would think an eternal hug sounded like a bad thing, too. 'THIS PLACE IS A BIT SCARY!'

The friends headed off in different directions in search of firewood. Amelia felt a little uneasy venturing through the Fairy Forest, but at least she had Squashy on her head for company. As she picked up a handful of sticks, her hand brushed something soft and fluffy. Amelia froze when she spotted a small pink ball of fluff. A fuzzmite.

'Uh, oh . . .' she whispered. She kept as still as possible. The fuzzmite stirred, but didn't appear to do anything.

Until . . .

CAZAAAAAR!

Within seconds the fuzzmite had grown ten times in size and developed an enormous face. Two giant fluffy arms protruded from its fluffy face, engulfing Amelia and nuzzling her into its soft cheek.

PA-DOING
PA-DOING

Eternal hug . . . Amelia thought. *This can't be good!*

'HEEEEEELP!' she yelled. But that made the fuzzmite squeeze her tighter.

Squashy bounced off Amelia's head and began to bounce on the creature's face.

The fuzzmite wailed and the hug tightened even more.

'Squashy, *stop*!' Amelia

wheezed. 'That's not helping!'

Just then she caught a whiff of something sweet, and a glittery pink mist began to blanket the forest floor.

And was that footsteps she heard?

'Florence, Grimaldi? Is that you?' Amelia squeaked.

The creature squeezed tighter still.

Amelia couldn't find the breath to shout out any more. Just when she thought every ounce of breath was about to be hugged out of her, the fuzzmite yawned and its grip loosened, until Amelia could wriggle free.

Squashy **pa-doinged** into her arms and the two looked on as the fuzzmite fell into a deep slumber.

Odd, thought Amelia. *That wasn't so eternal after all*.

The strange pink mist was getting thicker and began to surround her completely.

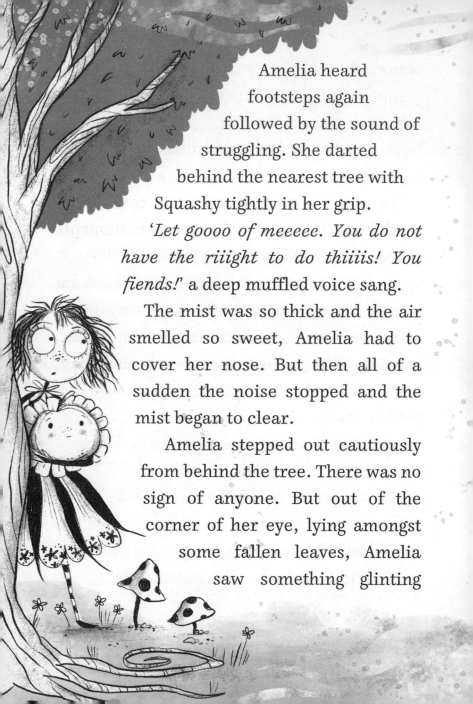

Amelia heard footsteps again followed by the sound of struggling. She darted behind the nearest tree with Squashy tightly in her grip.

'*Let goooo of meeeee. You do not have the riiiight to do thiiiis! You fiends!*' a deep muffled voice sang.

The mist was so thick and the air smelled so sweet, Amelia had to cover her nose. But then all of a sudden the noise stopped and the mist began to clear.

Amelia stepped out cautiously from behind the tree. There was no sign of anyone. But out of the corner of her eye, lying amongst some fallen leaves, Amelia saw something glinting in the light.

Squashy bounced over to the object and sniffed it.

'What is it?' Amelia asked, reaching down to pick it up.

The object was a smooth stick covered in sparkly jewels. At one end were some colourful feathers bunched together. Amelia picked it up and studied it carefully. She had no idea what it was or what had just happened.

Then the fuzzmite began to stir again. Quickly, Amelia placed the feathery stick safely up her sleeve and made her way back to her friends.

'YOU LOOK WORRIED,' said Florence as Amelia returned with a few sticks for the fire.

'Did you hear any distressed singing just now?' said Amelia.

'Distressed *singing*?' said Grimaldi. 'No . . .
I only heard Tangine's distressed moan as he
bumped into a tree trunk.'

'YEH, 'E WAS WELL RUBBISH AT
COLLECTING STICKS,' said Florence, poking
Tangine in the head. 'WENT ALL LAZYBONES
ON US!'

'I felt sleepy!' said Tangine.

'McSparkle was sleepy too,' said Grimaldi.
'He didn't help us collect even one stick!'

McSparkle shuffled on the spot. 'I told you,
I *wasn't* asleep!'

'YOU SO WERE, YOU BIG FIB-FACE,' said
Florence.

McSparkle picked up some sticks and
started to make a fire in the clearing.

'Did you happen to see any pink glittery
mist? Or smell anything sweet?' said Amelia.

'*Pffft!* No, thank goodness!' said Grimaldi.

'Strange,' said Amelia pulling out the

jewelled stick with the feathers on the end.

'Ooo, what's that?' said Tangine.

'I don't know,' said Amelia. 'I found it after I heard the singing and the mist disappeared.'

Tangine took the jewelled object and studied it. 'It's pretty,' he said. 'I want it!'

'No, Tangine,' said Amelia gently taking the stick back. 'It doesn't belong to you. Clearly somebody has lost it, so we'll keep it safe until we can find its owner.'

Tangine looked dejected, but didn't argue.

'Well, the fire's all set for the night,' said McSparkle stepping back from a pinky-yellow flame. 'Anyone else have the urge to skip round it merrily?'

Amelia and her friends stood in an awkward silence.

Three minutes later, everyone was skipping merrily around the fire.

And even though back home in Nocturnia everyone would be awake now, Amelia and her friends had had such a long day that ten minutes later, they were fast asleep.

CHAPTER 6

RAINBOOOOW!

At first light, McSparkle was singing.

'Uuuuup and at 'em!'

'I'LL UP AN' AT *YOU* IN A MINUTE!' Florence grumbled, forgetting where she was.

'What time is it?' groaned Grimaldi.

'It's sunrise, you silly sunflower!' sang McSparkle. 'C'mon now, time to head to the Vivid Valley to wait for the Rainbow Rail.'

The friends followed McSparkle through the Fairy Forest for what seemed like an eternity. Just as Amelia thought she couldn't go any further, the trees parted to reveal an expanse of pastel-coloured hills reaching as far as the eye could see.

'Vivid Valley is looking *extra vivid* today!' McSparkle trilled, stretching his arms out towards the lush scenery.

Amelia had never seen anything like this before. The colours were overwhelming. She was so used to greys and blacks. *This* was a feast for the eyes.

'I feel sick . . .' said Grimaldi, clearly struggling to handle the new spectrum of colours in front of him.

Tangine's mouth dropped open. 'It's *beauuuuutiful!*'

'No sign of the Rainbow,' said McSparkle. 'Hopefully it's not already been and gone!'

Amelia breathed in deeply. The air was a mixture of sweet, sparkly and fresh. She was starting to miss her mum's Slug Slime-Trail perfume after all.

As the friends followed McSparkle along

the length of Vivid Valley, Amelia noticed more and more Creatures of the Light gathering. Tangine spent the whole journey trying to catch any bumblebee that flew in his path. Unfortunately, he ended up with more stings than bees.

'No Rainbow yet?' McSparkle addressed a purple pony with a glittery tail.

'Not yet,' said the pony. 'Soon, though. I can feel it in me tootsies!'

'Excellent!' said McSparkle, rubbing his hands together. He turned to Amelia. 'Fancy a snack?' He pulled out a small pouch from his pocket and poured out some tiny red beans.

'LIKE THAT'LL FILL US UP . . .' commented Florence.

McSparkle started doing a little jig. Amelia couldn't help but giggle. He then stopped, clapped his hands three times, and . . .

POOF!

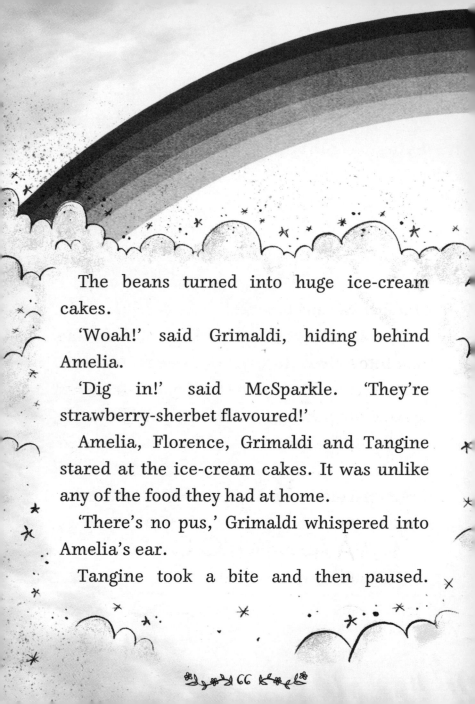

The beans turned into huge ice-cream cakes.

'Woah!' said Grimaldi, hiding behind Amelia.

'Dig in!' said McSparkle. 'They're strawberry-sherbet flavoured!'

Amelia, Florence, Grimaldi and Tangine stared at the ice-cream cakes. It was unlike any of the food they had at home.

'There's no pus,' Grimaldi whispered into Amelia's ear.

Tangine took a bite and then paused.

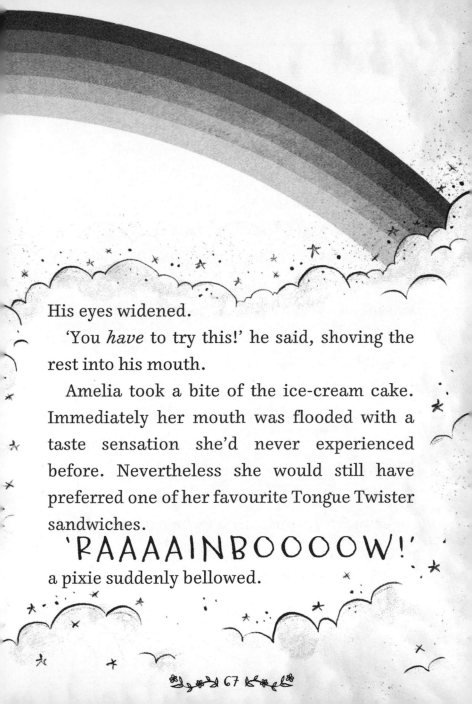

His eyes widened.

'You *have* to try this!' he said, shoving the rest into his mouth.

Amelia took a bite of the ice-cream cake. Immediately her mouth was flooded with a taste sensation she'd never experienced before. Nevertheless she would still have preferred one of her favourite Tongue Twister sandwiches.

'RAAAAINBOOOOW!' a pixie suddenly bellowed.

The Creatures of the Light cheered as a huge rainbow stretched across the sky.

Amelia felt the ice-cream cake fall out of her mouth as she gawped at the sight before her.

'Well, what're we waiting for?' yelled McSparkle. 'The Rainbow has arrived!'

Creatures of the Light began charging towards the end of the rainbow. Grimaldi squeaked with fear as the creatures swept past him.

Amelia held on to Squashy on her head and

made a run for it. 'Come on, guys! *To Glitteropolis!*'

The friends followed McSparkle, running as fast as they could. As Amelia got closer to the Rainbow, she saw a multicoloured train with an infinite number of carriages fading into the distance.

Suddenly, her foot caught on a small rock. With Creatures of the Light stampeding towards her, Amelia found herself crashing to the ground.

WOOOOOOOOOSH!

Florence swept Amelia up with one big hairy arm as a herd of noisy gnomes came thundering past.

Amelia breathed a sigh of relief, before realising that something wasn't right. She felt like a weight had been lifted from her shoulders, and not in a good way . . .

'Squashy is gone!' she yelled. 'He must have fallen off my head! Florence, turn back!'

With Amelia still in her arms, Florence span sharply on the spot and started to run against the crowd.

'Hey! What're you doing?' said a flying pig. 'The Rainbow is THAT way!'

But Florence kept running, pushing aside any Creature of the Light that got in her way.

'There he is!' Amelia yelled pointing at the confused pumpkin-daisy.

Squashy bounced up and down when

he saw Amelia, and pa-doinged straight into her arms. Florence quickly turned around and started running back towards the Rainbow.

Amelia gave a shriek. 'Oh no!' she cried. The Rainbow was already fading.

'*Hurry up!*' shouted McSparkle, as he jumped on to the Rainbow Rail and disappeared.

In the distance, from a carriage on the train, Grimaldi shouted, 'Quiiiiiick! The Rainbow's about to disappear!'

'What's taking you so loooooonnnnng?' Tangine called.

'BRACE YERSELVES,' said Florence, tightening her grip on Amelia. With one giant leap she hurtled through the air towards the end of the Rainbow. Amelia held on to Squashy and closed her eyes tight.

'I FINK WE'RE GONNA MAKE IT!' said Florence, stretching forward.

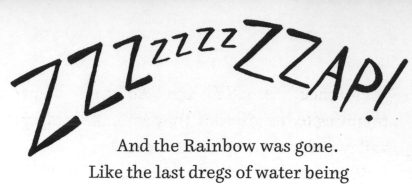

And the Rainbow was gone.
Like the last dregs of water being
sucked into a plughole.

Florence, Amelia and Squashy went tumbling to the ground. They sat in the empty valley and looked up at the clear sky.

'We missed it . . .' said Amelia.

THUD

DOING

CHAPTER 7
FABIO

'GUESS WE 'AVE TO WAIT 'TIL TOMORROW FOR THE NEXT RAINBOW,' said Florence.

'I'm sorry,' said Amelia sadly. 'It's all my fault. I hope Grimaldi and Tangine are OK.'

Florence put a big hairy arm around Amelia's shoulders. 'THEY'LL BE FINE.'

Squashy started bouncing up and down. **Pa-doing! Pa-doing! Pa-doing!**

'I'm sorry, Squashy,' said Amelia, looking at the ground.

Pa-doing! Squeak!

'WHAT'S UP, SQUASHMEISTER?' said Florence.

Pa-doing! Squeak! SQUEEEEEEEEEAK!

'MAYBE 'E NEEDS A POO,' Florence suggested.

SQUEEEEAK! SQUEEEEAK! SQUEEEEEEE EEEEEEEEEEAK!

'Squashy, what's wr—' Amelia paused as she looked up – then she gasped. 'The Rainbow! It's back!'

The Rainbow was stretching across the sky once again.

An echoey voice announced. *'Due to a fairy stuck in the toilet, the Rainbow Rail has been delayed by two minutes.'*

'WHAT'RE WE WAITING FOR? WE GOT TWO MINUTES,' Florence bellowed.

The friends ran as fast as they could towards the Rainbow and flung themselves into the nearest carriage.

DINGALING DING DONG

'Welcome aboard the Rainbow Rail! We sincerely apologise for the delay. The fairy has now been removed from the toilet. Please snuggle

up comfortably and enjoy the view as we make our way to our one and only destination . . . *GLITTEROPOLIS. We do hope you enjoy your journey with us todiddlyday!'* chimed the voice.

'WELL, THIS IS NICE,' said Florence, making herself comfortable on one of the carriage beanbags.

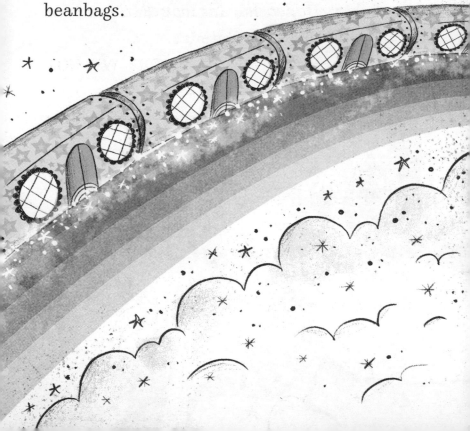

'Why, hello there . . .' said a deep voice.
Florence jumped and farted in fright.

A shiny young unicorn with a dark shimmery mane was perched on a nearby beanbag.

'YOU MADE ME JUMP,' said Florence.

'Apologies!' said the unicorn. 'I didn't mean to startle you. Allow me to introduce myself. I'm Fabio.' He swished his mane.

'FLORENCE,' said Florence.

'Lovely day.' Fabio smiled.

Florence peered out of the window and sniffed. 'AVERAGE, I GUESS.'

'So, where're you from?' said Fabio.

Florence shuffled uncomfortably in her beanbag. 'ERRRR . . .' she stammered.

'We're from Handsome Hill,' said Amelia stepping in. 'I'm Amelia, by the way. Nice to meet you.'

'Handsome Hill?' said Fabio raising an

eyebrow. 'I've never heard of it . . .'

Amelia felt a bead of sweat trickle down her forehead.

'THAT'S COZ IT'S A SMALL 'ILL,' said Florence.

'You're unlike any unicorn I've met before,' said Fabio, turning back to Florence. 'There's something different about you . . .' Fabio paused.

Amelia felt her heart pound in her chest.

'I know what it is,' Fabio finally said. 'Your mane – it's so full of life. How do you achieve that volume?'

Florence blinked at him, then looked over to Amelia who shrugged.

'ERRM,' said Florence, stroking her chin. 'S'ALL ABOUT THE CONDITIONER. CAN ONLY FIND IT IN 'ANDSOME 'ILL, Y'SEE. GOT EXTRACT OF . . . 'ILL.'

'Well,' said Fabio after a few seconds

silence, 'it looks beautiful.'

Amelia put a hand up to her mouth to stop herself from laughing. Florence's eyes widened.

'It's delightful to meet you, Florence,' said Fabio. 'Would you do me the honour of joining me for a Cuddly Custard Pie tomorrow?'

Florence sank lower into her beanbag and looked over at Amelia who was still trying not to laugh.

Before Florence could respond, Grimaldi, McSparkle and a rather bedraggled Tangine burst into the carriage.

'There you are!' puffed Grimaldi. 'We thought you were going to miss it a second time!'

'Lucky for you, your friend 'ere got stuck in the toilet!' said McSparkle. 'How he managed that I'll never know.'

'I was helping my *furmaids*!' said

Tangine defensively. He was wet and smelled strange.

'You could've just got stuck in the train door or something,' said Grimaldi.

Tangine gave Grimaldi a disdainful look.

'Hey there,' said Fabio, clip-clopping over to Grimaldi and Tangine.

'THIS IS FATSO,' said Florence.

'Oh, err, *no, no* . . .' said the dark-haired unicorn, 'I'm *Fabio*.'

'Good to see you again, Fabio!' said McSparkle, giving a friendly salute. 'Been anywhere nice?'

'Oh, you know,' said Fabio, 'the usual . . . Handing out leaflets about Glitteropolis in smaller towns.

Every creature

will be moving to the city in no time!'

McSparkle gave a little squee of excitement. 'Oh yes! And then we can finally live in peace!'

'Exactly,' said Fabio.

'I want a leaflet,' said Tangine.

Fabio smiled. 'It would be my pleasure. We must spread the Glitteropolis joy! Where are you from?'

Tangine stared at Fabio blankly. 'Um . . . I come from the lovely, errr, Misty Mountain Dew on a Summer's Morning Sparkle . . . Town?'

'That's my name,' said McSparkle frowning.

Amelia interrupted. 'Oh, don't listen to him! He's a real joker.' She poked Tangine hard in the arm. 'We're all from Handsome Hill! *Aren't* we?'

Tangine rubbed his arm, and Grimaldi nodded enthusiastically.

'Well, looks like we're arriving,' said Fabio.

'Here's the leaflet.' He handed Tangine a piece of parchment covered in glittery letters. Amelia felt her heart jump as she caught sight of the familiar words:

'GLITTEROPOLIS, the city where the sun never goes down, and your dreams always come true . . .'

The train began to slow. Outside the windows, a huge sugar-coated mountain range flickered into view and on the platform in huge glittery letters read the words:

WELCOME TO GLITTEROPOLIS!

CHAPTER 8
GLITTEROPOLIS

The train came to a stop and the doors slid open. Amelia sucked in a sharp breath, speechless at the sight before her. The whole city sat upon a huge swirly mountain, surrounded by pink clouds – a busy cluster of glittery houses, flowery market stalls and mini waterfalls. At the very tip of the mountain, a building that resembled a huge unicorn horn stood tall and glimmering in the bright sunlight.

Squashy bounced up and down next to Amelia, squeaking in awe.

'That view never gets old,' said Fabio, stepping outside. 'So, Florence, will you accept my invitation for a

Cuddly Custard Pie?'

'I DON'T FINK—' Florence began.

'She'd love to!' Amelia cut in.

Florence shot Amelia a stern look.

'Marvellous!' Fabio beamed. 'Meet me at the entrance to the FairyGround at noon tomorrow. We can get *extra* sprinkles!' And with that he galloped away gracefully.

'ERR, EXPLAIN?' Florence said to Amelia, folding her arms.

'Didn't you see?' whispered Amelia. She pulled out the scrap of glittery parchment from behind her wing.

'Look at the leaflet Fabio gave to Tangine! It matches the piece of parchment King Vladimir found just after Fairyweather's disappearance!'

'BUT 'OW DOES ME GOING TO GET A CUSTARD PIE CUDDLE WITH FLABIO 'ELP?' said Florence.

'I'm not sure
yet,' said Amelia,
'but it's the only lead we
have right now.'

Tangine wandered over, reading the
leaflet out loud.

'**GLITTEROPOLIS, the city where
the sun never goes down, and your
dreams always come true . . . If you
believe in only light, Glitteropolis
needs YOU . . .**'

'Most Creatures of the Light are moving
here,' said McSparkle. 'There's even talk of
the Rainbow Rail closing down for good!'

'What?' said Amelia. 'But how do you get in
or out if it closes?'

'You don't,' said McSparkle. 'All the
Creatures of the Light will be here in
Glitteropolis safe 'n' sound! No need to ever
leave!'

GLITTEROPOLIS NEEDS YOU!

As McSparkle led the friends into the heart of the city, the buildings became much taller. Amelia noticed a lot of posters stuck to the walls and most of them pictured a very broad unicorn with a purple mane.

'Isn't he amazing?' McSparkle said, catching Amelia staring at the poster.

''OO'S THAT?' Florence bellowed. Grimaldi elbowed her in the stomach.

'Alpha Unicorn always looks out for us,' continued McSparkle. 'He and the other unicorn lords keep this city running smoothly. He knows what's best for us.'

Amelia was unsure what to say. Grimaldi's tummy started to rumble.

'Hmm, I'm mighty hungry myself.' McSparkle smiled. 'I know a *great* place – The McPot o' Gold. They serve the best Shimmering Shandy! And I *do* believe the weekly angel-kitten show is on this afternoon!'

'Oh goody,' said Grimaldi flatly.

At The McPot o' Gold, Amelia sat munching on a bowl of Fizzling Flower Fruit Pops, wishing it were crusty toenails. Squashy looked down disdainfully from the top of Amelia's head. Grimaldi was slurping a sugar-loaded slushy and Florence chewed on some Twinkled Toasties. Tangine was hanging half out of the window trying to catch bees in his empty glass.

'YOUR BEE DAD ISN'T IN GLITTEROPOLIS,

REMEMBER?' said Florence through a mouthful of toastie.

'We don't know that. He could have flown here.' Tangine lurched forward as another bee buzzed by, and almost fell out of the window. Florence grabbed his wings just in time.

'I KNOW YOU'RE UPSET ABOUT LOSING YOUR DAD, BUT WE'LL FIND 'IM.' She patted Tangine's shoulder. ''E'S PROBABLY

'AVING A LOVELY TIME AS A BEE. NOW 'ERE, 'AVE A TOASTIE.'

Tangine took the half-munched Twinkled Toastie from Florence and grimaced. 'Thank you?'

While nobody was looking, Amelia fed Squashy small nibbles of food. He didn't seem bothered by the taste, but Amelia missed the Fang Mansion butler Wooo's home-made Armpit Sweat-shakes and Putrid Pus-filled profiteroles. She was also missing her mum and dad. Despite the count's crossword puzzle obsession and Countess Frivoleeta's need for all things to be perfectly groomed, they *were* still her family.

Suddenly, a tiny angel-kitten wearing a ruffled collar flew on to the mini stage at the front of the room, snapping Amelia out of her thoughts of home.

'I have some sad news,' the angel-kitten

announced in a squeaky voice. The crowd murmured and groaned. Another angel-kitten in a ruffled collar fluttered on to the stage. 'The star of our weekly show, Adonis the Almighty, is *missing . . .*' The murmurs grew in volume.

'He went to visit his Uncle Abdominus last weekend in a small town just outside the Fairy Forest, and was meant to return today,' said a third angel-kitten. 'But he hasn't come back.'

'The Creatures of the Dark strike again!' cried a majestic peacock.

'Tragic,' said McSparkle. 'If he *has* been kidnapped, that'll be the *fifth* Creature of the Light to be snatched!'

'Who else has disappeared apart from Fairyweather and your brother?' asked Amelia.

'Fairyweather's sister, Sherryweather, and Flavia the unicorn. They both went missing a few weeks ago,' said McSparkle. 'They'd gone for a morning picnic in the Meadow of Loveliness but never returned. All that was left was their picnic blanket.' He shook his head in disbelief. 'I'm just glad the unicorn lords are investigating. If anyone can track down the culprits, Alpha Unicorn can!'

Amelia and McSparkle's conversation was

interrupted by a large genie with a clipboard shouting across the room.

'Hey! You!' she bellowed, pointing at Grimaldi. 'Can you sing?'

'I-I-I—' Grimaldi stammered, looking down at his kitten disguise in a panic.

'GOOD,' said the genie. 'We need a fourth singer for the Angel-Kitten Quartet. You can step in for Adonis.'

'*What?*' Grimaldi shrieked, spitting his fifth mug of Sugar Slush everywhere.

'Pottering pumpkins!' Amelia squeaked.

'Amelia, what do I do?' said Grimaldi, trembling partly from fear, but mostly from the amount of sugar he'd consumed. 'I'm seeing three of you . . .' he moaned.

But before Amelia knew it, Grimaldi was being ushered by the genie on to the small stage.

'The angel-kittens have never missed a

show. This is what Adonis would want,' said the genie. The three remaining angel-kittens re-emerged carrying various strange-looking instruments.

One angel-kitten chimed a bell. Another bonged a huge gong. Then the whole group started playing a strange but catchy tune.

Grimaldi stood frozen to the spot, holding a microphone and a bongo.

'*SING. SING. SING. SING!*' the crowd chanted.

Grimaldi opened his mouth . . . then burped a cascade of pink sparkly bubbles, before collapsing on the angel-kitten with the small trumpet.

'Kitten down. Sugar coma,' called McSparkle.

'I think it's time to go,' urged Amelia.

CHAPTER 9

COLLAR DUSTER

Along the cobbled streets of Glitteropolis, a very tired Amelia dragged her feet behind McSparkle.

'Never fear, young Amelia, I know the perfect place for you all to stay. An eighty-four-star hotel with the best views in Glitteropolis. *Follow me!'* McSparkle called back.

Florence stomped along slowly carrying Grimaldi, who occasionally murmured *'sugar!'* Tangine, making use of his fairy wings, weaved in and out of the streets and swooped under and over the glitter-coated bridges.

'Here you go!' sang McSparkle as they

approached a tall pastel-pink building. Above the revolving door it read:

Welcome to The Syrup Slumberlands Hotel

'Thank you, McSparkle. You've been so kind,' said Amelia.

McSparkle blushed a little. 'Ah, shucks! Always here to help! Ooh, wait a minute . . .' He fumbled behind his ear and pulled out a ladybird with two very long curly antennae. 'Here, take this lucky charm!' he said, handing the bug to Amelia.

The ladybird buzzed and flew behind Amelia's ear, making her squeak.

'Lucky charms are the most reliable way to communicate in Glitteropolis,' explained McSparkle. 'Just tickle it between the antennae, say who you want to call, *and voila!* Go on, give her a try!' He ran around the corner out of earshot.

Amelia reached behind her ear carefully

and found the little bug perched comfortably. She felt between its two antennae and tickled its head gently.

'McSparkle,' said Amelia, feeling a little silly. The lucky charm began to buzz gently, making Amelia giggle, before she heard McSparkle's voice say, *'Hellooooo there!'*

'That's amazing!' said Amelia. 'How do I, err, turn it off?'

'Same way you turn it on!' McSparkle said with a chuckle. 'You can call me any time!'

'Thank you,' said Amelia as she tickled the lucky charm to end the call.

After several attempts to use the hotel's revolving door, the friends eventually entered The Syrup Slumberlands Hotel. They were greeted by an old and wrinkly fairy who showed them, very slowly, to a marshmallow-scented room.

Once they were alone, Florence sniffed the air. 'THERE IS NO WAY I'M GONNA SLEEP IN THIS STENCH,' she said.

'Perhaps we'll get used to it?' said Amelia, hopefully.

Florence had dumped Grimaldi on to one of the marshmallow beds. 'Argh,' he groaned. 'I have a sugar headache.'

Squashy gave him a suspicious sniff.

'WHAT A TURNIP,' said Florence. Then she wandered over to a huge screen on the other side of the room and pressed a big button at the bottom.

A bright, moving image of a galloping

unicorn suddenly appeared, making the friends jump. Tangine picked up a remote control and pressed a rainbow-coloured button at the top.

'Movies!' he said excitedly. 'I've never seen a movie . . . There's a *restricted* scary section. How about *The Goblin, the Beast and the Coffin*, or *Toad Wars*?' he went on, flicking through the film choices. 'Oh, how about *The Vampire King Strikes Back*?' Then he paused and sighed. 'I wish Dad was here,' he said.

The menu suddenly froze, as the words *BREAKING NEWS* flashed across the screen. A smart-looking unicorn with a curly blonde mane and a tie appeared.

'The Creatures of the Dark strike again as another member of our community has gone missing. Alpha Unicorn and the unicorn lords have confirmed that Adonis the Almighty,

star of *The McPot o' Gold's angel-kitten show*, has indeed been kidnapped. Alpha Unicorn advises Glitteropolans not to leave the safety of the city from now on. He has also confirmed that the Rainbow Rail WILL be closing, with the last trains to and from Vivid Valley tomorrow.

This is Eunice Eversprinkle on Glitteropolis Today, *wishing you light always*.

'Woah . . .' said Tangine.

'If we don't leave Glitteropolis before the end of tomorrow, we'll be stuck here forever!' said Amelia. 'We *have* to find Fairyweather before then!'

'I don't get it,' said Tangine. 'Who's kidnapping these creatures? *And why?*'

'It can't be the Creatures of the Dark,' said Amelia thoughtfully. 'They still don't know the truth and they'd run a mile at the sight of a Creature of the Light. Something odd is going on, but I don't know what it is . . .'

'WELL, WE AINT GONNA FIGURE IT OUT BEFORE BEDTIME,' Florence declared.

'You're right, it's late,' said Amelia. 'Let's get some sleep so we can get an extra early start tomorrow.'

'Good idea,' said Tangine with a yawn.

Grimaldi was already snoring.

Amelia, Florence and Tangine fell asleep to

the comforting screams and wails of *Toad Wars* playing on the TV in the background.

'Ergh, my head is all fuzzy,' moaned Grimaldi, rolling off his marshmallow bed the next morning. He clutched his head. 'I never want to eat or drink or *SMELL* sugar ever again.'

'Let's go, guys,' said Amelia. 'We have to try to find Fairyweather before the Rainbow Rail closes for good!'

Grimaldi began to breathe quickly.

'Don't panic,' said Amelia. 'We need to stay calm and focused. Florence is seeing Fabio at the FairyGround today – he might be able to help us.'

Amelia spotted a booklet called *The Sights and Sparkles of Glitteropolis* next to one of the marshmallow beds. It contained a map of the city. 'I'm sure they won't mind if we borrow this!' said Amelia, taking the booklet.

As the friends were struggling through the hotel's revolving doors, the fairy receptionist called after them. 'Wait! *Excuuuuuse me!*'

'OH MAN, SHE'S PROBABLY NOTICED THE MAP'S GONE,' said Florence, pushing at the door harder.

The revolving door span round at lightning speed, sending the friends flying back into the lobby, landing at the old fairy's feet.

Amelia looked up sheepishly. 'Um, hello . . .' she said. 'I'm really sorry for taking the map!'

'What're you talking about?' said the fairy. 'You forgot your collar duster!' She held up the jewelled stick Amelia had found in Fairy Forest. 'You want to be more careful with that. It's an expensive one.'

'Oh!' said Amelia. 'I must have dropped it. Thank you.'

After many more attempts at the revolving

door whilst the
old fairy watched
in amusement,
the friends *finally*
made it out of
the hotel.

'Collar duster?' said
Tangine looking at the
stick in Amelia's hand.
'As in, for *dusting* your
collar?'

Amelia shrugged. 'Beats
me,' she said. 'I guess that
would explain the
feathers,
though.
Who would
need one of *these*?'

As the friends
weaved their way

through the streets of Glitteropolis towards the FairyGround, Amelia spotted a small shop called Angel-Kitten Theatrical A-Mew-Sments. In the window was a glittery display of hats, jackets and ruffled collars. A hand-written sign read:

BUY TWO RUFFLED COLLARS –
GET A LIMITED-EDITION COLLAR DUSTER
FOR FREE.

Amelia took out the collar duster she had found and her brain began to whirl. Hadn't the angel-kittens at The McPot o' Gold been wearing ruffled collars?

'We need to find a newspaper!' said Amelia.

'How about that place?' suggested Tangine pointing at The Unicorner Shop.

Amelia ran in and found a stack of *The Curious Cloud* newspapers. The whole front page was dedicated to Adonis's disappearance. A picture of the star mid-song dominated the cover; one paw was on his chest, and the other was holding up a jewelled stick as if it were a conductor's baton.

Amelia's eyes widened as she stared at the picture. Her attention focused on his collar duster.

It was exactly the same as the one Amelia was holding.

'What's up?' said Grimaldi.

'I was there . . .' Amelia whispered. 'I was there in the Fairy Forest when Adonis was kidnapped. It's *his* collar duster that I found.'

CHAPTER 10
THE HAUNTED HOUSE RIDE

Amelia stared hard the picture of Adonis. She ushered her friends closer, and made sure the shop owner wasn't listening.

'Do you remember when we saw those Creatures of the Light in the Petrified Forest a few weeks ago? When we were trying to rescue Squashy?'

'Not really a forgettable experience . . .' said Grimaldi.

'HA! So, you DID trespass on the palace grounds!' said Tangine.

Florence glared at him. 'REALLY? YOU WANNA TALK ABOUT THAT NOW?' she growled.

'But, *of course,* that's in the past! All over. Done.' Tangine laughed nervously and looked down at his feet.

'Well,' Amelia continued. '*That's* the angel-kitten that approached me. It was *Adonis*!'

Grimaldi picked up a copy of *The Curious Cloud* and opened it, revealing a whole spread filled with pictures of the other missing creatures.

SHERRYWEATHER
LA FLOOFLE

LAVIA
LITTERBERG

'I recognise
her!' He pointed at
a picture of a unicorn.
Printed below was the name
Flavia Flitterberg. 'She's the
unicorn that turned my scythe into
a sunflower!'

Florence looked at the pictures of the missing

creatures and groaned. 'OH, MAN ... I FINK THAT'S THE FAIRY I SQUISHED,' she said, pointing at the picture of Sherryweather.

There was an awkward silence. 'I'm sure she's ... okay,' Amelia said reassuringly. 'But I wonder why they'd crossed the border into the Kingdom of the Dark?' she pondered aloud.

'Isn't it odd that all the creatures we saw in the Petrified Forest a few weeks ago have since gone missing?' said Grimaldi.

'Hmmm.' Amelia frowned. 'There's definitely something weird going on here.'

'Hey!' the unicorn shop owner called over. 'You gonna buy one of those newspapers or what?'

Amelia put the paper down. 'Come on, we need to get to the FairyGround to meet Fabio! It's the only way we'll get any answers,' she said.

The Glitteropolis FairyGround was buzzing with the hum of rollercoasters, the flashing bright lights of the rides and excited Creatures of the Light.

'LOOKS LIKE WE'RE EARLY,' said Florence. 'FABIO'S NOT 'ERE YET.'

'Hey, lovely Creatures of the Light!' said a flamboyant flamingo-dragon. 'Are you interested in winning free tickets to go on a ride of your choice?'

Amelia didn't really feel like going on a ride – her mind was racing and she was worried they were running out of time. 'I don't know,' she said. 'We're meant to be meeting a . . . friend.'

'All you have to do is make the bell ring by hitting the pumpkin with the rainbow hammer!' said the flamingo-dragon.

Amelia flinched. 'Hit the *pumpkin*?'

Squashy went pale, and squeaked nervously.

The flamingo-dragon pointed to a fake pumpkin model which looked more like a mutated potato.

'THAT'S NO PUMPKIN,' said Florence, poking the model. A small light rippled through

the pumpkin and up a pole connected to its behind, before ringing out:

'DONG DONG DONG! CONGRATULATIONS – YOU WIN! DONG DONG DONG!'

'*Fizzling feathers!* You did it!' said the flamingo-dragon. 'Nobody has ever managed to win before. You're certainly a *strong* unicorn.'

The flamingo-dragon handed over four glittery tickets, eyeing Florence up and down suspiciously. 'Well, enjoy your ride. You won fair and square!'

'COME ON,' said Florence. 'MAY AS WELL USE THESE TICKETS WHILE WE WAIT FOR FABIO. MIGHT BE FUN?'

'Ooo! A haunted-house ride!' said Tangine, pointing at a crooked mansion. 'That'll feel like home.'

Inside the haunted-house ride, the friends were strapped into a coffin-cart on wheels that rattled its way through the fake mansion. Creepy music was playing as they travelled along a dark corridor. Suddenly a robotic vampire burst out from a doorway.

'BLEEEEEH!' it shrieked, making a tiny unicorn in the coffin in front cry.

'*I VILL SUCK YOUR BLOOOOD!*'

'We don't say that!' Amelia scoffed. '*I hate blood!* It makes my breath stink!'

The robotic vampire opened its mouth, revealing a set of long, sharp fangs. It leant forwards, towards the crying unicorn. '*Mummyyyyyy!*' the unicorn screamed. 'Make the bad vampire go away!'

'It's just pretend, twinkletoes,' said the unicorn's mother.

'Are vampires really real, Mummy?' said the little unicorn.

'Yes, dear, but they can't hurt you in Glitteropolis,' said the mother. 'That's why Alpha Unicorn is closing the Rainbow Rail, to make sure those nasty creatures stay away from us.'

Tangine leant forward, clenching his fists, but Amelia placed a hand gently on his arm.

A group of young fairies were giggling on

the coffin-cart behind Amelia and her friends.

'I can't wait for the next bit,' said one fairy. 'It's the *SCARIEST*!'

The coffin-carts rolled along a rickety wooden track into a fake graveyard.

Dry ice filled the room and a rumbling sound was heard. A huge shadow appeared in the mist revealing a big hairy robotic yeti with ten eyes, three rows of pointy teeth and gigantic claws.

A little parp of glitter rose from the small unicorn's cart in front.

The fairies screamed and giggled. '*THE BEEEAASST!*' one fairy cried. 'It's so *UGLY! Quick!* It'll *crush your bones*!'

'ARGH!' Florence grumbled. Then . . .

BOSH!

But it wasn't Florence who had punched the robot yeti. It was Tangine.

The fairies in the coffin-cart started screaming as the robot yeti span out of control.

'Right in the hair,' Tangine said smugly.

CHAPTER 11
STRONG INDEPENDENT UNICORN

It was noon and Florence stood munching on a pile of Cuddly Custard Pies while she waited for Fabio. Amelia, Grimaldi and Tangine hid behind a nearby candy floss stand.

CLIP CLOP CLIP CLOP CLIP CLOP . . .

'Lovely day for it,' came Fabio's deep voice. 'I see you've already tucked into a Cuddly Custard Pie or four. Would you like another?' he asked.

'I'LL 'AVE ANOTHER FIVE. I'M STARVING,' replied Florence.

'Five pies for the lovely lady,' Fabio said to the pixie behind the counter.

'I AM NOT A LADY. I'M A . . . A . . .' Florence paused.

Amelia held her breath. Grimaldi put his hands over his eyes.

'I'M A STRONG, INDEPENDENT UNICORN,' said Florence at last.

Fabio looked at her blankly.

'She's going to give us away!' Amelia whispered to Grimaldi and Tangine.

They waited in anticipation as Fabio continued to stare at Florence. Then his face broke into a grin.

'Well, I *do* like a strong independent unicorn,' he said.

'AWFUL ABOUT THAT ANGEL-KITTEN'S DISAPPEARANCE,' Florence continued, licking the last of the five Cuddly Custard Pies. 'AND STILL NO SIGN OF FAIRYWEATHER

AFTER ALL THESE YEARS.' She sighed loudly. 'ANY IDEA WHAT'S GOING ON?'

Amelia put her head in her hands. Subtlety was not Florence's strong point.

'It's tragic,' said Fabio. 'When Fairyweather disappeared I was very young, but I remember it well . . .' He trailed off. 'But don't you worry about it,' he said, looking at Florence seriously. 'We unicorn lords have everything under control. My father has a plan!'

'YOUR FATHER?' said Florence.

'Alpha Unicorn,' said Fabio, raising his glittery eyebrows.

Amelia gulped and sat up straight. 'This is perfect!' she whispered. 'He'll definitely be able to help us find Fairyweather!'

Suddenly Amelia caught a whiff of something sickly sweet. It was a scent she had smelled before. It was coming from behind the FairyGround where the Unicorn Horn

Tower stood. As Amelia looked towards it she spotted a wisp of glittery pink mist float delicately up into the clouds.

'The pink mist!' She gasped.

'What are you talking about?' whispered Grimaldi.

'It's the pink mist I saw in the Fairy Forest just before Adonis was kidnapped!' said Amelia. 'And I recognise that sickly smell.'

'Ergh!' said Grimaldi, wafting the air.

'Veryyyyy odd,' Tangine said, stifling a yawn.

'Grimaldi, you stay here and keep an eye on Florence and Fabio,' said Amelia. 'Tangine and I will investigate!'

Amelia and Tangine weaved in and out of the market stalls that lined the park leading to the Unicorn Horn Tower.

As they approached the tower, Amelia noticed Creatures of the Light snoozing on benches and curled up in the middle of the cobbled path.

Tangine dragged his feet behind. 'Hurry!' Amelia urged.

'I'm trying,' said Tangine, 'but I'm super sleepy . . .' He yawned again.

Amelia spotted another wisp of mist rise from behind the tower.

'This way!' She and Tangine made their way around the side of the tower until they reached a huge gate with a sign reading:

· NO ENTRY – UNICORN LORDS ONLY ·

She heard shuffling, but she couldn't see what was going on through the mist.

Tangine slumped into a nearby bush head first, bottom up. 'What's *wrong* with you?' said Amelia, pulling at his leg.

'I waaaant thaaaaat ooooone,' Tangine slurred and yawned.

Amelia shook her head and groaned. The mist was getting thicker still.

Suddenly, Amelia spotted movement through the gate. She could just make out the outline of a cage. It looked like something was inside.

Then she saw it. The silhouette of a kitten – a kitten with a ruffled collar.

Amelia gasped, but swiftly covered her mouth as she glimpsed two unicorns wearing hooded cloaks walking towards the gate.

Dark masks covered their noses, which meant their voices were muffled, but she could just make out what they were saying.

'Put him in the candy chambers with the others,' said a deep voice. 'And *hurry*. We only released ten minutes' worth of slumber smoke! Fabio won't be happy if we're seen!'

'Of course!' said the other masked unicorn, bowing and walking away.

Amelia heard the creaks and turns of wheels on cobbled ground, and the silhouette of the kitten in the cage disappeared.

The candy chambers? Amelia wondered. Whatever they were, they didn't sound good.

'*Fabio . . .*' she muttered angrily under her breath.

CHAPTER 12

THE UNICORN BANQUET

Dragging a sleepy Tangine behind her, Amelia ran as fast as she could back to where Grimaldi was hiding. The pink mist was clearing from around them. Tangine slowly began to perk up, and was jogging along in tow.

Florence was still standing by the Cuddly Custard Pie stand, munching through yet more pies.

Fabio was nowhere to be seen.

'*Where* is that rotten sprout?' Amelia growled.

'FABIO 'AD TO LEAVE BUT 'E PAID FOR THE WHOLE STAND OF PIES SO WE CAN

EAT THE LOT!' said Florence, happily.

'I *bet* he had to leave,' said Amelia crossly. 'Did he happen to mention *where* he was going?'

'SAID IT WAS AN EMERGENCY. BUT 'E INVITED ME TO THE UNICORN BANQUET TONIGHT IN THAT BIG TOWER!' said Florence.

'Come on,' said Amelia. 'I need to tell you something. Somewhere we won't be overheard.'

The friends gathered in the haunted-house ride, hidden behind a broken down coffin-cart to the side of the tracks. Amelia knew nobody would hear them amongst the screams.

'I think I know where Adonis is! Which means Fairyweather and the other kidnapped creatures might be there too,' said Amelia. 'I think Fabio and the unicorn lords are behind the whole thing! They've been using something called slumber smoke to cover their tracks.'

'Is that the pink mist? It must send Creatures of the Light to sleep,' said Tangine. 'It even made *me* quite drowsy. I guess I didn't fall completely asleep since I'm only *half* Creature of the Light.'

'You're right, Tangine!' said Amelia. 'And that would explain why McSparkle was sleeping while we collected firewood in the Fairy Forest . . . *and* why the unicorn lords I saw were wearing masks.'

'Clearly it doesn't affect Creatures of the Dark,' said Grimaldi, jumping at the sudden appearance of the spinning yeti robot.

'BUT WHY WOULD THE UNICORN LORDS KIDNAP OTHER CREATURES OF THE LIGHT?' asked Florence.

'Maybe they found out about my mum and dad?' said Tangine, twiddling his thumbs.

'HMMM, THAT *WOULD* MAKE SENSE,'

said Florence. 'SOUNDS LIKE THE UNICORN LORDS LIKE BEING IN CONTROL. THEY PROBABLY WOULD 'ATE THE IDEA OF THE TWO KINGDOMS TALKING TO EACH OTHER.'

'Oooo, oooo!' said Tangine. 'Because *that* would mean they'd find out the *truth* about each other!'

Amelia frowned. 'And if the Creatures of the Light weren't scared of the Creatures of the Dark any more, the unicorn lords wouldn't be able to control them.'

'To be honest, if I were scared and I didn't know any better, I'd look to the unicorn lords for comfort,' said Grimaldi. 'They're always promising to keep the Creatures of the Light safe from danger.'

Amelia nodded, deep in thought.

'Florence, you said Fabio invited you to the unicorn banquet tonight?' said Amelia. 'I'll come with you. Adonis was sent to the candy chambers which must be *somewhere* inside the Unicorn Horn Tower. Hopefully that's where we'll find Fairyweather and the other missing creatures.'

'UMM, BUT FABIO TOLD ME IT'S UNICORNS ONLY AT THE BANQUET,' said Florence.

'Well,' said Amelia. 'Time to put our creative skills to the test!'

Somehow Amelia, Florence and Grimaldi managed to transform Amelia's fairy costume into a unicorn outfit. Tangine rolled up the leaflet Fabio had given him to make a cone-shaped horn for Amelia to place on her head.

'Squashy, you'll have to stay with Grimaldi and Tangine, okay?' said Amelia, hugging him into her chest. Squashy squeaked and waggled his stalk bravely.

'THE BANQUET BEGINS WHEN THE DAILY PINK PARROT SINGS,' said Florence.

The friends stared at Florence blankly.

'IT'S WHAT FABIO TOLD ME, ALRIGHT?' she huffed.

'Well, good luck!' said Grimaldi. 'We'll wait here in the haunted house for you!'

'We'll get your mum back, I promise!' Amelia said to Tangine.

'WE GOT THIS,' said Florence, giving Tangine a friendly nudge.

Tangine nudged her back, and then threw his arms around Florence's hairy belly. 'Thank you for being a lovely *furrrriend*,' he said.

Florence patted Tangine on the back awkwardly, and then cleared her throat.

'ERR, THAT'S ALL RIGHT.'

Amelia and Florence crept out of the comforting dark of the haunted house and into the daylight.

FAAAAAH LA LA LAAAAAAAAAA! sang a pink parrot as it flew across the bright blue sky.

'It's time!' said Amelia. 'Let's go!'

Amelia and Florence joined a stream of extravagantly dressed unicorns making their way to the Unicorn Horn Tower. Huge iron gates stretched high into the sky.

The gates creaked open and two unicorn guards stepped forward.

'NAMES?' one guard shouted.

'FLORENCE   AND . . . ERRR . . .' Florence   paused.   'FLORENCE'S LITTLE SISTER.'

The unicorn guard unravelled a scroll, which fell to the ground and carried on unravelling. He looked at Amelia and Florence suspiciously.

'I don't see your names on here,' he said.

Amelia sensed Florence's

whole body stiffen.

'FABIO INVITED ME,' Florence replied.

The unicorn guard carried on scanning the guest list.

The other guard leant over and whispered something. Amelia wiped her damp palms on her unicorn suit.

'Oh . . . you're right, Ricky!' He pulled out a pair of half-moon glasses from his top pocket and popped them on to the

tip of this nose. 'Can't see a thing without these!' He laughed. 'Oh, look. There you are, Florence!' he said, then pulled out a pink pen with a pom-pom on the end and crossed the name off. 'No mention of your sister, though.'

The unicorn guard called Ricky glanced at the scroll. 'You're right, Graham.'

'REALLY?' said Florence, then she leant in towards the guards. 'IT'S ME SISTER'S BIRFDAY, SHE'S BEEN SO EXCITED ABOUT THIS.'

Amelia looked up at the unicorn guard called Graham and gave him her very cutest smile.

'Aww,' Graham cooed, 'happy birthday, little one! Go on in and have fun!'

With sighs of relief, Amelia and Florence walked through the gates and made their way into the Unicorn Horn Tower.

❈ CHAPTER 13 ❈

FLORENCE'S UNIQUE TALENT

Inside, Amelia and Florence were led into the Hall of Horns. A table ran along the front of the hall, with a large, imposing throne at its centre. Careful not to draw attention to themselves, Amelia and Florence sat down at one of the smaller round tables near the back of the hall.

'Florence!' Fabio galloped over, wearing a long glittery cloak. 'Oh, and you are?' he said, looking at Amelia.

'THIS IS ME LITTLE SISTER,' said Florence. 'SHE WANTS TO BE A UNICORN LORD WHEN SHE GROWS UP.'

'How nice. You never mentioned you had a sister,' said Fabio. 'You do look strangely familiar, though,' he said to Amelia, frowning.

'THAT'S COZ SHE LOOKS LIKE ME, SILLY!' Florence laughed nervously.

Fabio didn't look convinced. But then, luckily, they were saved by the bell.

DONG. DONG. DONG. DONG!

'Let the banquet commence!' yelled an old bearded unicorn at the front of the hall.

Loud cheers rang out as five unicorn lords in glittery cloaks strode to their seats at the front of the hall. They were followed by a huge, purple-haired unicorn with a long jewelled cape.

It was Alpha Unicorn. Fabio made his way to the front and stood next to his father.

'Greetings!' began Alpha Unicorn. 'It is a pleasure to have you here at a very special unicorn banquet!' He looked slowly around the room. 'I have some marvellous news . . . The Rainbow Rail *will* be closed for good after tomorrow's midday ride from Vivid Valley, and the citizens of Glitteropolis WILL BE SAFE FOREVER MORE!'

The whole room cheered.

'Glitteropolis is *almost* impossible to find. But with the Rainbow Rail there's always a *tiny* chance an unwanted creature might find its way in. Without the Rainbow Rail we'll be safe from the rest of the world . . . safe from the *wrath* of the Creatures of the Dark!' yelled Alpha Unicorn.

'It's about time!' shouted an orange-maned unicorn.

Fabio gazed admiringly at his father and the crowd erupted into clapping and hoof pumping.

Amelia shuffled closer to Florence for comfort.

Alpha Unicorn
suddenly looked serious.
'Those vampires will *suck*
your blood! Those vultures
will tear you to shreds,
those BEASTS WILL
CRUSH YOUR BONES!'
Florence stood up so quickly
her chair nearly toppled over.
'I AM NOT . . .' she paused.
The room went silent.
Amelia felt her heart
almost stop.
Florence swallowed.
'. . . GOING TO PUT UP
WIV THAT ANY LONGER!'
'Yeeeeahhhh!' the crowd
rumbled.
Alpha Unicorn bashed
the table with a polished

hoof and the room went silent. 'I, Alpha Unicorn, will keep *you* safe,' he said. 'The sun will never go down in our city and all of the Creatures of the Light will prosper! GLITTEROPOLIS. NEEDS. YOU!'

The crowd were stomping, cheering and clapping. One unicorn fainted with happiness.

'We're going to have to join in the celebrating,' Amelia whispered to Florence.

'BUT IT FEELS SO WRONG.'

'Everything about this is *wrong*, but if we don't pretend to be happy, we're going to give ourselves away!' said Amelia.

'*WHOOP WHOOP!*' shouted Florence – but just a little too late. The crowd had already calmed down and now every eye in the room looked at her.

'Is that *your* guest, Fabio?' said Alpha Unicorn.

'Yes,' said Fabio. 'Father, meet Florence.'

'Hello, Florence,' said Alpha Unicorn. Amelia could feel her cheeks burning as everyone stared at them. 'I am so delighted that you could join us tonight. And do tell me, Florence, what is your unique talent?' Alpha Unicorn raised his eyebrows. 'As we all know, *every* unicorn has a *unique* talent.'

Amelia felt a flicker of panic run through her bones. *A unique talent?* she thought. She wasn't entirely sure what Alpha Unicorn meant by this, but she was quite certain *pit digging* wouldn't be an acceptable answer.

Florence didn't react. The silence in the hall was deafening. Amelia couldn't read Florence's expression. She had no idea how they would get out of this sticky situation . . .

'SONG,' Florence suddenly blurted out.

'*Song?*' Amelia repeated.

'Song?' said Alpha Unicorn. 'Very well. How about you demonstrate your song?'

This is it, thought Amelia, *this is the part where they find out who we really are* . . . Florence stood up and cleared her throat. Amelia couldn't bear it any longer. She lifted her knees up to her chest, hugged them tight and closed her eyes. *I'm so sorry, Tangine,* she thought. *We tried . . . We really tried . . .*

Then Amelia heard a sound so pure and hypnotic, all her troubles seemed to drift

away. The sound filled the hall with a mesmerising melody. She lifted her head slowly and saw Fabio's eyes widen and Alpha Unicorn straighten up. The sound was every beautiful thing you could imagine all rolled into one. It was as if a spell had bewitched the whole room.

And this sound was coming from Florence's mouth.

It was the most exquisite song Amelia had ever heard. It seemed every unicorn in the room was in a complete trance, captivated by its magnificence.

Amelia's mouth gaped open. She'd had no idea that Florence could sing so beautifully. But she couldn't stay and listen any longer – this was her chance to find Fairyweather and the other kidnapped creatures! She needed to slip away while the crowd was distracted.

As she tiptoed out of the room, not a single unicorn looked in Amelia's direction. *Keep singing, Florence*, she thought.

CANDY CHAMBERS

CHAPTER 14

THE CANDY CHAMBERS

Amelia stood in a long corridor lined with framed portraits of unicorns staring into the distance. A sign on the wall read 'Corridor of the Courageous'. Amelia cautiously made her way down the corridor until she spotted another metal sign engraved with the words CANDY CHAMBERS. But the sign was underneath a painting of Alpha Unicorn standing on a cliff looking thoughtful.

That's odd, thought Amelia. She couldn't see a door or any way in.

Suddenly she heard voices which seemed to come from behind the wall. Amelia looked from side to side for a place to hide. Spotting a door labelled PRINTING ROOM, she quickly slipped inside.

Peering through a small crack, she saw the painting of Alpha Unicorn swing forward. The two unicorn guards she'd met at the entrance gate emerged.

'Alpha said the Memory Flush is ready, so we can test it first thing tomorrow morning,' said the guard called Ricky.

What in Nocturnia is a Memory Flush? Amelia wondered.

She held her breath and waited until the clip-clopping of their hooves disappeared.

She was about to step back in to the hall when she turned to take a quick look at the room she'd been hiding in. In front of her sat hundreds upon hundreds of coverless textbooks on conveyer belts connected to a huge printing press. Amelia picked up a book and her breath caught in her throat.

'The Wrath of the Angel-Kitten,' she read. It was one of the books studied at Catacomb Academy, that warned them about how scary and dangerous Creatures of the Light were. On the other side

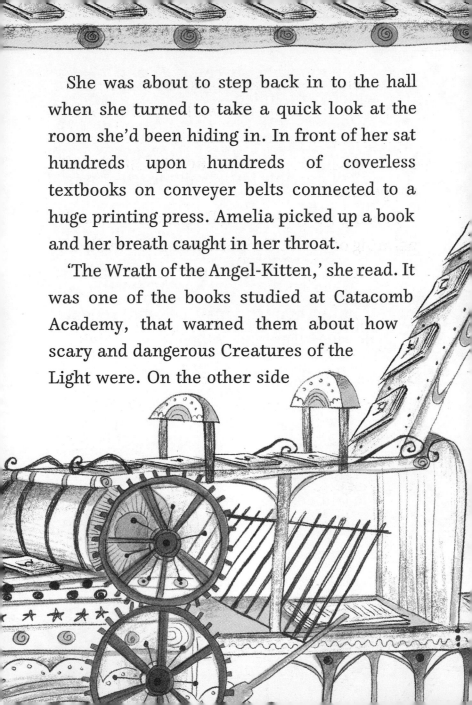

of the room she saw another pile of books which included *Vicious Vampires: Volume 1*, *The Beast that Lurks* and *The Gruelling Truth About Ghosts* – no doubt full of horrible lies about the Creatures of the Dark.

Every single book had the same author: Dr Alfayewny Kawn.

'Doctor Alfayewny Kawn,' Amelia read aloud. Then she paused and repeated slowly, 'Doctor Alfayewny Kawn ... Yewny Kawn ... *Unicorn! Alpha Unicorn!*' Amelia gasped. '*He* has been creating all of the books about us – and spreading all the lies.'

But time was running out. She had no idea how long Florence could keep the unicorns distracted. She had to get to the candy chambers.

Making sure there were no more guards

lurking around, Amelia tiptoed up to the painting of Alpha Unicorn and carefully pulled it open. Sure enough a long staircase stretched into the darkness. Amelia walked down, as quickly and quietly as she could, until she reached a huge metal door framed by frosted cakes and stripy sweets. Above the door was a sign that read:

WELCOME TO THE CANDY CHAMBERS

Amelia pushed the door open slowly and peered into a room that looked like an enormous sparkly prison made of sweets.

Two rows of chambers with shiny candy cane bars, one on top of the other, lined the walls. A fairy flew up to the

stripy bars and shouted, '*You won't get away with this!*'

Even though the fairy was clearly angry, her voice was soft. She stared at Amelia with her big eyes. She looked sad. She was small, but not tiny, perhaps the length of an adult's arm, and her hair was sparkling white.

Behind the bars, the fairy frowned. 'You're an odd-looking unicorn,' she said. 'Are you a new guard?'

'Not exactly,' said Amelia. She felt nervous, but she wasn't sure why. Slowly, she removed her unicorn disguise and stepped into the light.

'You're . . . a vampire?' said the fairy. She didn't seem scared of Amelia, just slightly confused. 'Who *are* you?'

Amelia suddenly realised why this fairy wasn't scared of her. This was the same fairy she'd seen in King Vladimir's scrapbook of memories.

It was Tangine's mother, Queen Fairyweather La Floofle.

Amelia smiled. 'I'm Amelia Fang. I'm a friend of Tangine, and we've come to help you escape.'

Fairyweather's eyes widened and she took a step backwards. 'You know my son?' she whispered.

Amelia nodded. 'We travelled from Nocturnia to Glitteropolis to find you.'

'You did?' said Fairyweather breathlessly. 'But Glitteropolis was built so that it would be almost *impossible* to find . . .'

'Well, it *was* for a while,' said Amelia. 'A long while. King Vladimir spent *years* looking for you.'

Fairyweather bowed her head. 'My dear husband,' she said quietly. 'How is he?'

'Um,' Amelia began. 'He could be better . . .' She paused. 'But he'll be *much* happier once you're home.' Amelia didn't feel it was the right time to tell Fairyweather that her husband was currently a bee.

'Oh, sparkling,' said Fairyweather looking a little more hopeful. 'I want nothing more than to go home to my family – but how are we going to escape this place? The unicorn lords will surely see us.'

'Well, we got *in*, so we can get *out*!' Amelia grinned.

A rosy-cheeked leprechaun skipped up to the bars of the next chamber and punched the air joyfully. 'A good determined lass you are!'

'You must be McShine!' said Amelia, shaking the leprechaun's hand. 'Your brother helped us find Glitteropolis.'

'Ah, my brother's a gem. I've missed him!' said McShine, tipping his hat.

'Oh, it's *youuuuu! Cooooo-eeeeeeeee!*' said another fairy, waving from the candy chamber above McShine. She was *much* smaller than Fairyweather, with a higher voice. 'I'm Sherryweather! We've met before! In the Petrified Forest that time.'

'Oh yes! I recognise you,' said Amelia, waving back.

'I think you were a bit scared, though,' said Sherryweather, 'and then your friend *nearly* squished me.'

Amelia put her head in her hands. 'I'm so sorry about that. Back then, we still believed fairies stole vampires' fangs! We were terrified of you,' she said, blushing.

Sherryweather laughed and flapped a hand. 'Oh, don't worry, sweetpea! In fact, I've been wanting to *thank* your yeti friend. She sorted my bad back *right* out!' she said, twirling around on the spot.

Amelia smiled weakly. 'Oh well, that's good! I'm glad you weren't . . . *completely* squished.'

'We used to travel to your kingdom every night just before sunrise to try to find King Vladimir,' said Sherryweather. 'We wanted to tell him what had happened to Fairyweather, but there was never any sign of him.'

'He was either looking for her in the Kingdom

of the Light or hidden away in the palace,' said Amelia sadly.

'When we spotted you and your friends, we thought we might try to communicate, but we should have known you'd probably be too scared of us,' said Sherryweather kindly.

'I tried to *sing* you the truth about what had happened,' said another, deeper voice, 'but I got *wafted* away. One does not appreciate being *wafted*.'

An angel-kitten in a ruffled collar appeared in another candy chamber.

Amelia gasped. 'You must be Adonis! I think I found something of yours.' She pulled the jewelled collar duster out from her sleeve and passed it through the bars to the little angel-kitten.

'*Glittering gibbons!*' said Adonis, taking the collar duster. 'My prized possession! My collar is *so* dusty right now I thought I might die, you know—'

'Oh, Adonis,' Fairyweather said with a twinkly laugh, 'you're such a drama cat.'

'I am an *actor*, sweetling! *I'm famous*!' he said in a theatrical voice.

'Famously *annoying*,' said another voice.

Amelia looked across the room to another dark chamber. A beautiful rainbow-haired unicorn stepped into the light. Amelia recognised her from the newspaper.

'Flavia!' Amelia beamed. Flavia bowed her head.

'I still can't believe you found us, Amelia,' said Fairyweather.

'I promised Tangine we would find you,' Amelia replied. 'And friends don't break promises. He needs you, Fairyweather.'

'Ever since I met Vladimir and realised the truth about our two kingdoms, I wanted to bring the Creatures of the Light and the Dark together,' said Fairyweather. 'But somehow, the unicorn lords found out about us and they kidnapped me. Since then, they've hunted down anyone who knew the truth.'

'Well, we will *show* those unicorns—' Amelia began, just as the candy chambers' doors burst open.

'Show those unicorns *WHAT*?' shouted Fabio.

❀ CHAPTER 15 ❀

FLORENCE IS NOT A BEAST

'I knew it!' Fabio spat. 'IMPOSTER! You're not a unicorn *at all*!'

Florence came running in close behind. 'I'M SORRY, AMELIA,' she said. 'EVERYTHING WAS GOING FINE, THEN WHEN I FINISHED SINGING I 'AD GAS AND I BELCHED. APPARENTLY REAL UNICORNS CAN'T BELCH!'

The two unicorn guards charged in, dragging a very big wriggly sack.

'LET US OUT!' came Tangine's voice.

'Help, Amelia!' cried Grimaldi from inside.

'Found these two lurking around the

haunted-house ride trying to catch bees!' said the guard called Ricky. Then he caught sight of Amelia and screamed. 'Aaaaaargh! Vampire! Graham!' he called to the other unicorn guard. 'It's a vampire! Get it before it sucks our blooooood!'

'VAMPIRES DON'T SUCK BLOOD!' shouted Florence. She pulled off her unicorn horn.

'Twinkling Tootsies!' cried the guard called Graham. 'It's a *BEAST*!'

'Florence is *not* a *BEAST*!' Tangine shouted as he burst out of the sack, followed by a cloud of bees. 'She is a RARE BREED OF *YETI*!'

Fairyweather gasped at the sight of her son, and fell to her knees.

'*Tangine?*' she called.

Tangine looked over at Fairyweather and froze.

'Tangine,' his mother repeated. A glittery tear rolled down her cheek.

Tangine didn't move. Grimaldi poked his face out of the hole made in the sack to see what was happening.

'M-Mum?' stammered Tangine at last, taking a step towards Fairyweather.

'It's me, Tangine! *It's me!*' she cried and stretched her arms through the candy-striped bars.

Tangine ran full pelt towards his mother's chamber and grabbed both of her hands tightly.

'Oh, Tangine!' said Fairyweather. '*My son!*'

'*WHAAAAAAAAT?*' Ricky and Graham gawped.

'Can someone *please* explain what's going on here?' said Graham.

Tangine bowed his head. His voice broke as he muttered, 'Mum, I can't believe it's really you . . .'

He leant his forehead on to Fairyweather's and closed his eyes.

'I never thought I'd see you again!' Fairyweather wept.

'ENOUGH!' said Fabio, dragging Tangine away from her and into a candy chamber on the other side of the room.

'You'd better join him in that chamber – and keep quiet – otherwise Fairyweather is FAIRY TOAST,' said Fabio to Amelia, Florence and Grimaldi.

Silently, they did what they were told.

'GUARDS! Keep watch!' said Fabio. 'My father will decide their fate.'

He galloped out, leaving a nervous Ricky and Graham keeping watch.

Amelia scowled at them both before something caught her eye from behind one of the huge sparkly pillars. She craned her neck but nothing was there. Had she imagined it?

But when she looked again, her heart leapt. There, peeking out, was a little orange pumpkin dressed as a daisy.

❊ CHAPTER 16 ❊

A TICKLE BEHIND THE EAR

Amelia beckoned Florence and Grimaldi over. 'Grimaldi, I need you to distract the guards. I have an idea!'

'Okay, I'll do my best.' Grimaldi removed his angel-kitten ears and tail to reveal his own black cloak. With one waft, he floated up to the chamber bars and sighed loudly.

'ARGH!' shrieked Ricky, stumbling backwards. 'Ooh, he made me jump, Graham!'

'He can't hurt us from behind those bars, Ricky,' said Graham. 'Don't worry.'

'I have something to tell you,' said Grimaldi casually.

'Hush, evil Creature of the Dark!' warned Ricky.

'Oh, okay. I guess you don't want to know your fate then?' said Grimaldi.

'Don't listen to him, Ricky,' said Graham.

'But Graham,' Ricky whispered, 'he said he knows my *fate*!'

'He's a *Creature of the Dark*,' Graham exclaimed. 'He's trying to trick you.'

'But what if he's not, Graham?'

The two unicorn guards bent down. 'Tell us, dark creature, what does my future look like?' said Ricky.

Grimaldi pretended to think carefully. 'You must keep extra still so that I can read your fate.'

While the unicorns were focused on Grimaldi, Squashy silently rolled across the floor. Then, very carefully, he grabbed the keys dangling from Ricky's belt with his mouth, and swallowed them whole. *GULP*.

'Hey!' said Ricky turning and pointing at Squashy.

Amelia froze.

'Graham,' he went on, 'what did I tell you about bringing flowers into the candy chambers? You know I'm allergic!'

Squashy kept as still as possible. Graham bent down so that his nose was level with the little pumpkin. 'I don't remember doing that, Ricky. And besides, what a strange daisy that is. And I know my daisies.'

Then, without warning, Squashy bit Graham's nose with an almighty *CHOMP!*

'*AAAAAAAAAAAAAARGH!*' Graham cried.

While the two unicorn guards danced around and fell over each other in a panic, Squashy bounced up to Amelia and burped out the keys. Amelia swiftly unlocked the chamber and ran out, picking up Squashy on her way. Graham rolled around on the floor holding his nose.

'Oi!' shouted Ricky. 'Get back here!' He picked himself up and galloped towards Amelia.

'I GOT THIS!' said Florence. She stood between Amelia and the unicorn guard so that Amelia could unlock the other chambers. As Amelia freed the other prisoners, she tickled the lucky charm behind her ear. '*McSparkle*,' she whispered, 'I hope you're listening . . .'

'Move it, *BEAST*!' said Ricky.

'WHEN ARE YOU GONNA GET IT INTO YER FAT 'EAD . . . I AM NOT A BEAST!' Florence roared. 'I'M A RARE BREED OF *YETI*!'

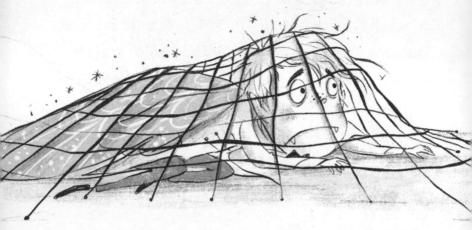

Across the chamber, Tangine sped towards his mum. But, before he could reach her, a giant sparkly net landed over him. Amelia watched as her friend was dragged across the room to the doorway, stopping at the hooves of Alpha Unicorn.

'Now, now, *now*, what *do* we have here?' Alpha Unicorn said, peering down at Tangine.

'Don't you lay one hoof on my son!' yelled Fairyweather, flying across the room. Another

sparkly net sent her crashing to the ground.

'*Mum!*' Tangine shrieked.

'Oh, now *this* is pure gold,' said Alpha Unicorn. 'I KNEW you'd been hanging around with vampires, but you kept *this* quiet,' he said, pointing at Tangine. Alpha Unicorn lowered his head until he was eye level with him.

'You are no Creature of the Light, nor are you a Creature of the Dark,' Alpha Unicorn sneered. 'You do not belong *anywhere*!'

'Don't talk to our friend like that!' said Amelia.

Adonis swooped down and landed on his back two paws next to her. *'This is unacceptaaaaaaable!'* he sang dramatically, waving his collar duster in the air.

'Yeah!' screamed Sherryweather, spin-flying across the room.

'Quiet, fairy!' sneered Alpha Unicorn.

McShine cartwheeled between the guards and then jigged aggressively towards Alpha Unicorn who looked on, unimpressed.

'You're not gonna defeat us again, you big bully!' said McShine.

'Is that so?' said Alpha Unicorn flatly.

Tangine bowed his head. He looked defeated. 'I don't care what you do to me,' he muttered. 'Just let my mum go.'

'And why should I listen to *you*?' said Alpha

Unicorn. 'You're an *abomination*.'

'My son is no different from you or me,' cried Fairyweather. Then she stopped and broke into a smile. 'Actually, I take that *back*. He *is* different . . . He's *better* than you!'

'Do not speak to my father in that manner!' said Fabio, stepping out from behind Alpha Unicorn.

'You're such a *creep*, Fabio,' said Flavia, strutting over to join Adonis, Sherryweather and McShine.

Fabio walked up to Flavia slowly until his nose was almost touching hers.

'I expected better from you . . . *sister*,' he sneered.

Amelia gasped.

'You can still be one of us, Flavia,' said Alpha Unicorn, turning from Fairyweather. 'You don't have to do this. You were born to be so much more!

You're a Creature of the *Light*! You're a *unicorn*. Look at your *perfect* city. Why would you want to ruin it?'

'It's not perfect, Father,' said Flavia. 'You lie to your citizens. You invent stories to make them scared of the Creatures of the Dark!'

'She's right,' said Fairyweather, 'the Creatures of the Dark aren't dangerous and they are certainly not evil. There's no reason why the two kingdoms should be divided. Think of all the wonderful things we could do *together*!'

'That will never happen!' spat Alpha Unicorn. 'As long as both kingdoms are scared of each other, I am in control!'

'You wrote all the books we read at school,' said Amelia, remembering her discovery in the printing room. 'Why would you write books that lie about your own kind?'

'Teaching each kingdom to fear the other is

the key to my success as ruler of this city. If you fear us, you stay away. Simple. But *some* of my own creatures were still determined to break the rules . . .' Alpha Unicorn glared at Fairyweather. 'Wandering beyond the border into the Petrified Forest after hours, and trying to communicate with the Creatures of the Dark! I cannot have you telling the rest of my kingdom *the truth*. You leave me only one option.'

'Ooo, oooo! *I* know!' said Ricky, with his hoof in the air.

'It's the Memory Flush, right? *Right?*'

Alpha Unicorn's shoulders slumped. 'You totally *ruined* my evil reveal,' he said, narrowing his eyes.

'Oops, sorry,' said Ricky. 'But . . . *Am I right?*'

'I think it's time I put my top-secret plan into action,' Alpha Unicorn continued. 'It's time for . . .' He puffed his chest out.

'He's totally going to say Memory Flush this time!' Ricky said excitedly.

Alpha Unicorn glared at the guard. 'Get out.'

Ricky walked out of the candy chambers with his tail between his legs.

'As I was saying. It's . . . MEMORY-FLUSH TIME,' bellowed Alpha Unicorn.

'What do you mean, *Memory Flush*?' asked Flavia.

'Allow me to explain,' said Alpha Unicorn,

slowly circling Amelia and her friends. 'Your brains will be flushed through and you will not remember *anything*. You won't even remember each other. So, enjoy your last moments together.'

Alpha Unicorn laughed maniacally as a huge, multicoloured contraption was lowered from the ceiling.

'You can't do this,' cried Fairyweather. 'I can't believe you'd erase your own daughter's memory!'

'She's better off this way,' said Alpha Unicorn. 'Come on, Fabio. Let's activate the Memory Flush *together*.'

Fabio gave the friends an evil grin and followed his father towards the candy chambers' exit.

Amelia took a deep breath and hugged Squashy tightly. Florence and Grimaldi held hands. Fairyweather and Tangine embraced through the holes in the nets that still held them. Flavia, Adonis, McShine and Sherryweather bowed their heads and linked arms.

This was it.

But just as Alpha Unicorn and Fabio approached the exit, Ricky burst back through the doors, breathing heavily. From behind him came a rumbling sound.

'I thought I told you to *leave*!' said Alpha Unicorn.

Ricky caught his breath. 'I tried to stop them, sir . . .'

CHAPTER 17

LEPRECHAUNS, ASSEMBLE

From behind Ricky, an almighty herd of Creatures of the Light exploded into the candy chambers. McSparkle was at the helm, riding upon a swarm of ladybirds.

'*YAHOOOOOO!*' he cheered. 'Me lucky charms never lie! But it appears *you* do, Alpha Unicorn!' he shouted. 'Yeah, that's right. We heard EVERYTHING!'

The assembly of Creatures of the Light caught sight of Amelia, and skidded to a halt.

'*VAMPIIIIIRE!*' screamed a flying pig, and the herd turned to run back out again.

'They're harmless though!' said a genie.

'We heard the truth!'

The crowd turned back, brandishing their croissants and various baked weapons of choice. But then they paused mid-run once again as a bunny rabbit screamed, '*Gaaaah! It's gonna crush me toes!*' pointing at Florence.

The herd prepared to scurry out of the door for a second time.

'But they're on *our* side!' a ladybird squeaked.

Everyone started forward again.

'DEATH!' squealed a twinkling star, looking at Grimaldi with big wide eyes.

But this time everyone just looked a bit unimpressed and carried on into the candy chamber.

'All right,' said McSparkle, 'we're all here. Sorry about that. It's just gonna take a bit of getting used to the Creatures of the Dark, after being terrified for so long!'

Amelia smiled. 'It's okay, we felt the same when we first met you,' she said.

'As soon as I heard what was happening through me lucky charm, I contacted as many creatures as I could,' said McSparkle. 'And we broadcast the truth across the whole network of ladybirds.'

McShine stepped forward. 'ME BROTHER!' cried McSparkle. Amelia thought they were going to go in for a hug, but they ran towards each other, then linked arms and danced a reel.

'The truth about the *lies* is *out*!' said Grimaldi. 'Wait, is that right? Or is it the lies about the truth? I'm confused.'

'Outrageous!' said Alpha Unicorn. 'Guards! Lock them *all* up!'

Graham looked at the sea of creatures in front of him. 'But, sir, there aren't enough chambers . . .'

'Then Rainbow Flush them all!' said Alpha Unicorn.

'Father, we're trapped – there are too many of them blocking our way out,' said Fabio. He looked around desperately as a group of angry leprechauns surrounded him and Alpha Unicorn.

'Leprechauns . . . . *ASSEMBLE!*' they cried. The mob of leprechauns pounced, forced Alpha Unicorn and Fabio into the nearest chamber, then locked it with a flourish.

McSparkle broke free from the commotion and skipped up to Amelia, tipping his hat. 'Y'know, you look better without the fairy wings – you suit being a vampire much more.' Then he bowed. 'Thank you, Amelia, for revealing the truth to us all.'

Amelia blushed. 'Thank you for believing us,' she said with a smile. 'Oh, and here . . .' She tickled behind her ear and out flew the lucky charm ladybird McSparkle had given to her. 'You might say it works a *charm* . . .'

'You keep it,' said McSparkle. 'Then we can stay in touch!'

The crowd cheered and Daisy-Squashy pa-doinged into Amelia's arms and then settled cosily on top of her head.

Amelia held hands with Grimaldi and Florence, who put a big hairy arm around Tangine.

Fairyweather flew over to Amelia. 'I can't thank you enough for bringing Tangine and I together again.'

'AND ONCE KING VLAD'S NOT A BEE ANY MORE, EVERYFING WILL BE JUUUST SWELL,' said Florence.

'A *bee*?' said Fairyweather, looking confused.

'OH . . . YOU DIDN'T KNOW YET?' said Florence. 'WELL, THIS IS AWKWARD.'

Fairyweather looked blankly at Amelia, then burst out laughing. 'My husband as a bee . . . Now that I have *got* to see!'

'She's not angry?' Grimaldi whispered to Amelia.

'WE CAN EXPLAIN,' said Florence.

'Oh, my sweetlings, it's okay,' said Fairyweather. 'I'm sure it's nothing that can't be fixed.'

Fairyweather bowed her head. She then opened her wings and slowly rose above the crowd.

'It's time to unite the Kingdoms of Light *and* Dark once and for ALL!

I, Queen Fairyweather La Foofle of the Kingdom of the Light, with King Vladimir of the Kingdom of the Dark, will make sure you are FREE to live wherever you wish!'

The candy chambers exploded with cheers.

Ricky and Graham stood awkwardly at the side of the dungeon. 'I did not see this coming,' said Ricky.

'Y'know, Ricky,' said Graham. 'I'm kinda tired of being a guard. The hours are too long. I've always wanted to travel.'

'Me too, Graham – maybe I'll join you!' said Ricky. 'How about a trip to Nocturnia?'

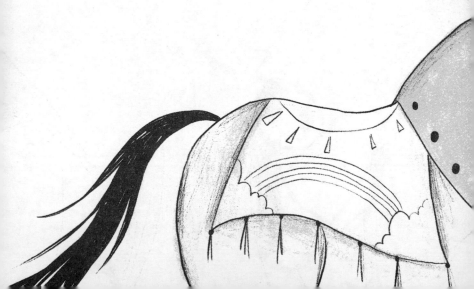

CHAPTER 18

LIGHT AND DARK

'. . . And then Florence and Adonis did this amazing duet – you should have heard it, Mum! And we went outside and danced until we all fell asleep. The sun never ever goes down in Glitteropolis, so we had no idea what time it was. I think we danced for two days solid!'

It had been a few nights since Amelia and her friends – along with Queen Fairyweather – had returned to Nocturnia. Amelia was still recounting tales of their adventures to her proud parents. King Vladimir was back to being a vampire – Fairyweather had found bee-Vladimir in the Bug Blossoms near the

Meadow of Loveliness, and used a wish at the well to change him back.

'Darling, I knew it was you straight away,' she said, laughing. 'You were the only bee trying to build a honeycomb palace.'

'Well, I had no idea how long I'd be a bee, so I thought I'd make it feel like home,' he said. 'I tried talking to Tangine to tell him I'd wait in the Bug Blossoms but I could only buzz.'

Queen Fairyweather and King Vladimir sat together at the head of the long dinner table in the Nocturnia Palace Dining Hall. Since they had been reunited, they hadn't left each other's side.

Countess Frivoleeta had been a little wary of Fairyweather when they first met, but once Fairyweather complimented her frills, the countess warmed to her.

'You know, we could do something positively disastrous with your hair!' said Countess

Frivoleeta, admiring Fairyweather's ringlets. 'I have a frightful collection of hairpieces in my horrifying-hair room back at the Fang Mansion. We could try them out and make you look just like *me*!'

The countess was so excited that her left eyeball popped out, making a PLOP sound as it landed in Fairyweather's plate of Spaghettied Spleen.

Fairyweather scooped up the eyeball with her spoon. 'Eye eye, countess!' she said, chuckling.

The king burst out laughing but it came out as a loud *BUZZZZ*. 'Oops.' He blushed.

'Still a few lingering bee habits.' He pulled out a jar of honey from inside his cloak. 'Dig in, everyone – I made it myself!'

Amelia never thought she'd see the day when vampires, yetis and grim reapers would be sharing a celebratory dinner with Creatures of the Light.

Amelia sat next to Tangine and Florence, who was munching on a platter of Sparkled Skin Shreds and Deadly Drizzled Donuts. The Fangs' ghost butler, Wooo, the Mummy Maids from the palace, and Sherryweather – who was quite the chef – had all worked

together to combine some delicious Light and Dark dishes.

Count Drake was happily engrossed in a new Glitteropolis-themed crossword puzzle.

'Oh, Fairyweather,' said King Vladimir softly, 'I still can't believe we're together again.'

'It's a miracle, my gorgeous little glitter puff,' said Fairyweather. 'If it wasn't for Amelia, Squashy, Florence, Grimaldi and our son, I may never have seen you again.' She smiled at Amelia and her friends.

'And if it wasn't for Amelia, Squashy, Florence, Grimaldi and our son I'd never have made the best honeycomb castle the bee community ever did see either!' replied the king.

Fairyweather flew up to him and perched lovingly on his shoulder. 'To friends!' she declared.

Amelia grinned at Tangine. 'To fur-riends!'

'Exactly,' Tangine agreed, raising a glass of sugar-loaded slushy with mischief in his eyes. 'To FUR-MAIDS!'

And everyone burst out laughing.

Suddenly McSparkle and McShine skipped into the room playing fiddles.

'Are you ready, folks, for an angel-kitten show like no other?'

Grimaldi, Adonis and Flavia strutted into the dining room, each wearing a ruffled collar. Grimaldi had dressed in his angel-kitten costume for the occasion. Amelia giggled and began clapping in time to the music. And Squashy pa-doinged in, dressed as a daisy once again.

'He's so cute!' Flavia squealed, then licked Squashy on the belly.

After much dancing, laughing and a few too many sugar-loaded slushies and Shimmering

Shandies, Queen Fairyweather clinked her glass and called out above the music.

'Tangine, my sweetling, your father and I have something we wish to give you.'

Tangine's eyes lit up and he ran over to his parents. 'You do?'

'Since I've not been around for any of your birthdays, I wanted to make it up to you . . .' Fairyweather looked to her husband. 'Your father told me about your little phase of being a spoilt sprout.' Tangine blushed and twiddled his thumbs. Florence gave his shoulder a friendly squeeze. 'And how you *really* wanted a pet . . .' Fairyweather continued.

A Mummy Maid walked in carrying a huge golden box tied up with an orange ribbon. 'Happy *birthdays*!' said Fairyweather.

Tangine didn't say a word. Florence poked him. 'Th-th-thank you,' he stammered, pulling the ribbon loose with a shaky hand.

As soon as Tangine opened the box . . .

PA-DOOF

A huge pumpkin landed on the table top with a thud.

'A pet pumpkin!' shrieked Tangine.

Squashy bounced cautiously on to the table. The two pumpkins stared at each other in

silence. Amelia picked Squashy up and rubbed his tummy reassuringly. 'I'm sure you'll get used to each other.'

Tangine tried to pick up his new pumpkin – but he was too heavy.

'He was in the genetically modified section,' said King Vladimir. 'Nobody buys those poor things. But we thought you'd like him.'

Tangine looked as if he might cry. 'I . . . *love* him!' he said and gave the big pumpkin a hug. 'I'm going to call him *Pumpy*!'

Pumpy bounced up and down – *THUD THUD THUD* – making the cutlery clatter and the glasses topple over.

'Well,' said King Vladimir, 'I think it's time you all went to bed. The grown-ups have lots of important things to discuss now that the Kingdoms of the Dark and the Light will be coming together!'

Tangine folded his arms and raised his

eyebrows. 'Really, Dad? We all know you're just going to play Dungeons and Daymares.'

'Oh, *are* we now?' said Fairyweather, folding her arms too.

The king looked at his wife and smiled sheepishly. 'You will *love* it, darkling.'

Amelia felt her heart swell as she watched Tangine and his family laugh together.

As Amelia lay in her coffin that day, with Squashy snuggled up beside her, she thought about how lucky she was to have friends like Florence, Grimaldi and Tangine. She was looking forward to sharing the kingdom with lots of new creatures too. And if she'd learnt anything from all of this, it was that Cuddly Custard Pies really weren't that bad, especially if you coated them with a sprinkle of Foot Flakes and Soggy Sweat Syrup.

THE END

Or is it. . .

There's somebody
lurking in the
shadows.
But who could it be?

Find out in . . .

AMELIA FANG
and the
MEMORY THIEF

Ravishing Rose Petal Rolls

Ingredients:

200g ground rose petals
125g sparkle syrup
5 unicorn tears
A puff of glitter
A drop of vanilla essence
Rainbow sprinkles

Method:

Skip round a glittery bowl, adding sparkle syrup to the ground rose petals, a spoonful at a time.

Fold the unicorn tears into the mixture until you hear angel song and it has turned every colour of the rainbow.

Add a puff of glitter and a drop of vanilla essence and then bake for twenty minutes until the rolls sprout with roses.

Shower with rainbow sprinkles and enjoy with some jolly jam and colourful custard.

Have you read all of
Amelia's amazing adventures?

She won't bite!

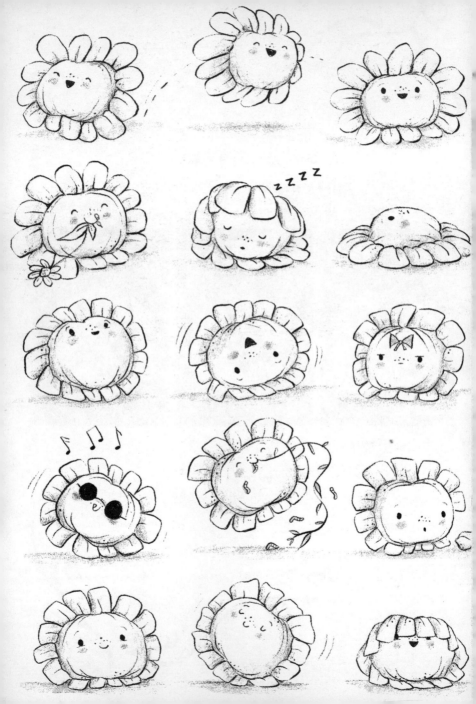